Scratch

AND THE PIRATES
OF PARADISE COVE

Scratch
AND THE PIRATES
OF PARADISE COVE

Ricardo Means Ybarra

PIÑATA

BOOKS

PIÑATA BOOKS
ARTE PÚBLICO PRESS
HOUSTON, TEXAS

Scratch and the Pirates of Paradise Cove is funded in part by grants from the City of Houston through the Houston Arts Alliance and by the Exemplar Program, a program of Americans for the Arts in Collaboration with the LarsonAllen Public Services Group, funded by the Ford Foundation.

Piñata Books are full of surprises!

Piñata Books

An imprint of
Arte Público Press
University of Houston
452 Cullen Performance Hall
Houston, Texas 77204-2004

Cover design by Mora Des!gn
Cover illustration by Giovanni Mora
Inside illustrations by Emmanuel Noe Nevarez & Mora Des!gn

Ybarra, Ricardo Means.
    Scratch and the Pirates of Paradise Cove / by Ricardo Means Ybarra.
    p.   cm.
    Summary: On the first day of summer vacation, ten-year-old Rafi and his father are searching for their lucky, six-toed cat, Scratch, when an earthquake knocks them off a cliff and they find themselves on a pirate ship, heading toward adventure.
    ISBN: 978-1-55885-525-0 (alk paper)
    [1. Pirates—Fiction. 2. Cats—Fiction. 3. Fathers and sons—Fiction. 4. Hispanic Americans—Fiction. 5. Adventure and adventurers—Fiction.] I. Title.
    PZ7.Y28Scr 2008
    [Fic]—dc22
                                                          2008016139
                                                          CPI

∞ The paper used in this publication meets the requirements of the American National Standard for Information Sciences—Permanence of Paper for Printed Library Materials, ANSI Z39.48-1984.

8 9 0 1 2 3 4 5 6 7   10 9 8 7 6 5 4 3 2 1

For Cynthia, *corazón* of love
and kindness.

1

I GUESS YOU COULD SAY it all started when I found the cat in our mailbox. He's not just any cat, but one so black and thin he could crawl into our mailbox, turn around inside and sleep there. I call him Scratch because of what happened when I found him. That was about six months ago.

I had gone out to the mailbox, pulled down the lid like I always do, and without looking inside, reached in to get the mail. Something furry lightly touched me on the top of my hand. It scared me so much I slammed the lid of the mailbox shut and jumped back about five feet. I thought it was a spider that had crawled on my hand. I looked at the top of my hand and could barely see four thin little scratch marks. Maybe it was a huge tarantula and I had tarantula fang marks on the top of my hand. I had barely escaped. I was really afraid but I had to see what had attacked me, so I snuck up as quietly as I could, pulled the lid open real slow, and scrunched up my eyes so I could see into the mailbox. It was real dark in there, and of course Scratch was black so I couldn't really see him. I was thinking to myself, "I'd better go into our mobile home and get the flashlight," when I saw his paw come out of the dark and stretch in the sunlight at the edge of the lid. Was I ever surprised, I wanted to touch him, but would you put your hand into a mailbox taken over by a strange black cat?

Of course, he hadn't really clawed me, just kind of touched me friendly like. I looked at the top of my hand again. The fang marks had already disappeared. I picked up a twig and gently touched the top of his tiny paw just like he had touched my hand, and you know what he did? He played with the twig. First he tried to grab it with his one paw, and then out came the other paw. His quick, grabby motions were so funny I started to laugh. That was when I saw his face. He had the cutest little saucer face I had ever seen, and then I noticed his paws. He had an extra toe on each paw, like a thumb. My dad says that it's a sign of good luck. And it is! I feel real lucky that Scratch adopted us.

2

SCRATCH LIVES WITH US now in our mobile home. We live in a trailer park at the beach, and that crazy cat still likes to crawl into our mailbox, or any mailbox, for that matter. So after I get up this morning on the first day of summer vacation and can't find Scratch, I'm not worried because I know where to find him. Usually I'd run outside to get Scratch, but my dad has french toast ready, and since I love french toast, I think Scratch will just have to wait. Besides, I always make sure to leave the lid of the mailbox open every night just so Scratch can crawl inside whenever he wants. Dad says I worry too much, that he's a lucky cat, but we have a lot of coyotes running around here at night, and I can hear owls too. At least I think he'll be safe inside our mailbox.

"*Mi hijo*," Dad says to me as we're eating our french toast. It sounds like "*mijo*" because he says it so fast. It's Spanish and it means "my son." My dad always calls me "*mijo*" or "Rafi" or "Rafito," although my name is Rafael.

"What are you going to do on your first day of summer vacation?" he asks me.

"Me and Matt are going boogie-boarding," I answer.

"Matt's mom is going to take you guys, right?"

"Right," I answer. "We're going to Pier Beach," I add. Matt and I love Pier Beach because there's no rocks and the sand is smooth. What we really like to do is run and jump on our boogie boards and slide across the wet sand into the water. It's better than riding waves. Besides, we're only ten years old and the waves look really big to us.

"Be sure to take a towel and the lunch I made for you. Don't forget to be polite," he says, making his eyebrows arch up.

"Yes, Dad," I answer as I carry my plate up to the sink.

"Well, I'm sure everything will be okay. Matt's mom has my work number. You have a fine first day of vacation," he says to me as he opens the sliding glass door to leave.

I look at my dad in the doorway. He's wearing shorts because it's summer. He kinda looks funny in shorts, you know how adults look. He's tall, and he has a big back and big arms from construction work and surfing. He tells me not to worry all the time, that I'll be as tall or taller than him, that he didn't grow until he was in high school. I hope so, because I'm almost the smallest and skinniest kid in my class. His hair looks even darker and curlier with the sun at his back. It looks like he forgot to comb it even though he did, and he needs to shave. He says he likes to shave every couple of days, but sometimes I wonder. I wave and say, "See ya when you get home. Don't worry, Dad."

But he doesn't leave. He leans in and asks me, "You need anything else?"

"No. Well. . . . when am I going to Mom's?"

"Tonight. We'll leave after dinner, all right?" Then he shuts the door and I can hear his pickup truck start, and I watch him drive down the narrow street crowded with mobile homes.

I'm glad he's gone because now I can do whatever I want. It's kinda fun to be alone in the house. But not that alone. The first thing I'm going to do is go out and bring Scratch in to play with me. I run outside to the mailbox. I notice that the lid is shut, which is okay because Scratch doesn't seem to mind, but he's not inside. I try not to worry, but I get a squeaky feeling in my stomach as I run to the back of our mobile home and can't find him in his other hiding place under the lime tree. Matt will help me find him, so I yell to Matt over the wood fence that separates our mobile homes. When Matt doesn't answer I hop on my bike and ride around to the street behind ours where Matt's mobile home is. It's funny that he's already getting on his bike to come over to my house, as if we had the same exact idea.

"Hi, Matt," I yell.

"Hi, Rafi. I was just coming over to your house. What are you doing?" Matt answers. Matt is much bigger than I am, and blond. He gets burned in the sun a lot faster than I do because his skin is so white, and he has real short hair. Sometimes I wish that my hair was blond instead of brown, but I wouldn't want it short. My hair is kind of long and wavy, especially in the back. I'm really glad that my skin is brown so I don't have to worry about sunburns so much, but I do wish I was bigger, like I told you before.

Matt calls me "Rafi" because he says Rafael is too long of a word to say all the time. He's my best friend, and he's an awesome bike rider. I look at Matt and notice that he's wearing red sweat pants like me. It's funny; sometimes we think alike.

"Matt, you have to help me find Scratch. He's not in my mailbox and I haven't seen him since last night when he wanted to go out." I say this while riding around in a tight circle. For some reason I can't stop or stand still. Matt doesn't seem worried. I hope he'll help me.

"I bet I know where he is, Rafi. Remember that time we found him in the iceplant behind the basketball court?" Matt says.

"Yeah," I answer over my shoulder as I ride around him. "Come on. Let's ride down there."

Matt hops on his bike and we race around the corner and down the hill to the basketball court. The basketball court is in a gully off the main road in the mobile home park. People may think living in a mobile home park is dumb, but this place is great. It's called Paradise Cove, and we have a basketball court and fields to play ball, and of course, the beach is right at the end of the dirt fire road, which is also the greatest place to skid tires. The people who live in the park are real nice too. Dad says it's like a village, that he doesn't have to worry too much when I'm left alone for a while because everyone watches out for me.

We skid to a stop by the backstop and I drop my bike and start running. I have to wait for Matt because he always puts down his kickstand.

"Matt, hurry up," I yell. I know right where Scratch's hiding place is and beat Matt there. Matt's puffing when he reaches me. Like I said, he's a lot bigger than I am.

"Did you find him?" he asks, breathing hard. I look at him nervously and start to rub my hands like I do when I'm upset.

"We gotta find him," I tell Matt in a scared voice, and feel myself wanting to cry. I stop myself, thinking that maybe Dad is right; I worry too much.

"Are you all right, Rafi?" Matt asks. "Are you gonna cry?" I'm not mad at Matt because he

knows me real well, practically better than anyone except for my mom, and I know he's not
trying to hurt my feelings, but I sort of yell at him
anyway, maybe because I don't want him to know
I'm scared. "No, I'm not going to cry. Scratch is
just out playing somewhere." I do want to cry a
little because I am scared and I don't want anything to happen to that silly black cat and no one
is at home to help me, but I don't. I don't like to
cry. I wish that my mom didn't live in another
house over the hill and that my dad wasn't at
work.

"It's gonna be all right, Rafi. My mom'll help
us. Don't worry; we'll find Scratch. Come on,"
Matt says. He starts to run down through the trees
to the bikes. I feel better already and take off after
him, but I trip on one of the roots that bump up
under all the pine needles. "Oooh," I grunt as I
land on my stomach and hands and feel needles
and dust spreading over me like a wave at the
beach. I can feel the dust all over my face, so I
squint my eyes and shake my head before I get
up. That's when I see it.

"Matt, come back here. You gotta see this. It's
rad." I don't forget about Scratch, but I can't
believe what I just found, and anyway, it was
because of Scratch that I found it.

"What is it? It better be good, Rafi," Matt says.

"Oh, yeah. Wait'll you see this," I say as I hold up the weirdest gold coin I have ever seen so it'll shine in a ray of sunlight coming through the tree branches. We both stare at it.

"Oh, man, that's so cool. Where did you find it?" Matt's sweating he's so excited.

"Right here. It was right under my eyes and I saw it when I fell," I say, and then I start to laugh because Matt is laughing too. I rub the coin on my T-shirt so it shines up real nice and we both look at it carefully. It's kind of rough, not perfectly round, and it has strange markings on it. A cross with a dot in each corner, and on the other side there's some funny writing and a shield.

"It's so cool, dude. Let me hold it, Rafi," Matt says, reaching out for the coin. I don't want to hand it over at first, but I remember that he's my best friend so I drop it in his palm. Matt acts like he's afraid to touch it, as if it were hot. He doesn't touch it with his fingers. Finally, I take it back from him.

"You should see your face. It's black," he says, laughing really hard and pointing at my face which makes me laugh even harder. "Come on," he says. "Let's go find Scratch. That coin is awesome. Do you think it's real gold?"

"Yeah," I answer. "Doesn't it look like a pirate's coin? Hey, Matt, maybe there's a buried treasure here." My voice is higher than the tree

tops, but I don't think Matt hears me. He's already running back down to the bikes.

"Come on, Rafi. We gotta get back to my house. My mom's waiting for us. There's no buried treasure here. This is a mobile home park. That's just a cool coin. Come on. Are you coming? We gotta find Scratch."

I guess he did hear me, but he's getting on his bike. I stick the pirate coin in my shoe and hurry on my bike to catch up with him.

3

MATT'S MOM DRIVES US around the park and we even look in other mailboxes, but we can't find Scratch. I want to call my dad at work but Matt's mom says to wait, you know how adults are, so I don't have a very good time at the beach even though the waves are small and the wet sand is perfect for sliding.

Matt's mom drops me off at our mobile home late in the afternoon. I want Matt to stay with me until Dad comes home, but his mom says he has to go shopping with her. After they leave, I go into my room to play a game on the computer my grandfather gave to me for Christmas, but I can't concentrate very well, so I turn it off. I call my mom to tell her about Scratch and see if she'll come over to help me, but all I get is her message machine. I leave her a message about Scratch that ends with, "Mom, you gotta come over and help me find him. Call me as soon as you get home. Bye. I love you." Then I wait for Dad to come home. It seems like I have to wait forever. The afternoon passes as slowly as the last day of school.

Finally I hear Dad's truck pull into the driveway, and I am out and at his door before he has a chance to turn the engine off. I hold onto his door and try to speak calmly, but it all blurts out.

"Dad, I can't find Scratch. I'm so worried about him. You have to help me find him. Can we drive around and look for him? Please, Dad?"

Dad looks at me quietly for a second and asks, "Can I clean up first?" But then he says, "Sure, hop in." I climb over him. I know he would have liked to take a shower because he's dirty from working. My dad is a tile-setter. He says he loves his work and he doesn't mind that he gets so dirty because then a shower feels so good.

He backs out and we drive around the streets of our mobile home park. I lean out the window calling, "Scratch," and "Here, boy," but we don't see him anywhere or hear his cute meow. I am feeling so sad when Dad parks in our driveway, but then he has a great idea.

"Why don't we get on our bikes and go look for him? But first, I need a shower. Okay, *mijo*?" he asks me.

"Yeah, Dad. I'll get your bike ready," I tell him. I feel much better. As soon as I hear the water running in the shower I run out the back door and wheel his big bike to the front of the house. Then I have to wait again, but not for long because Dad is a quick shower-taker.

We get on our bikes and start searching on our street first. I look in everyone's mailbox. I hope no one thinks I'm trying to steal their mail.

We don't find him on our street, so we ride down past the basketball courts into another section of the mobile home park. I'm starting to get real worried. The sun is going down, the wind has picked up, and the seagulls are making a very sad sound as they fly over us.

After we search that section of the park and even ask everyone we see if they have seen a skinny black cat with one extra toe on each front paw, we end up at the bluff overlooking the ocean. There's a four-foot-high chain-link fence at the edge to keep people from falling off. It's a good thing, because it looks like it's about three hundred feet to the beach below, although Dad says it's only a hundred feet. "That's far enough!" I think. We park our bikes and walk over to the fence to look over the side.

"It's beautiful here," I hear Dad say but I don't think it's so beautiful right now, without Scratch. I lean my chin on the metal rail at the top and rub it hard so that it makes my teeth push against each other. It hurts a little, but then it sort of feels good too, if you know what I mean.

"You're really shooting up," Dad says.

"I guess so," I answer sadly.

"We'll keep on looking for Scratch," he says, rubbing my shoulder, trying to cheer me up. "Maybe he's out playing. He might be back at the mobile home right now. Race you back."

But I don't move. I don't feel like racing. I'm just so worried.

Then, just as Dad says the words, "You ready?" and tickles me on my sides the ground starts shaking.

"Oh my God, it's an earthquake," Dad shouts, picking me up and trying to run away from the cliff's edge. But we don't make it. All I really remember is the ground shaking and us falling over the edge, and I can see the beach below so clearly it seems that I can count every rock and every piece of driftwood on it. I hear Dad shout something in my ear, but I can't understand him because the air is rushing past my face so fast, and then I feel something smooth and slick catch me just like at the bottom of a slide. It's all white and soft.

4

IT ISN'T THE BEACH. It's a sail! I've fallen into a huge sail. I don't remember seeing any sailboats when I looked over the edge of the bluff, but here I am. Then I see Dad sliding down the sail and stopping right next to me.

"Where are we, Dad?" I ask excitedly, happy that we aren't hurt. "What happened to the earthquake?"

Dad scratches his head. I can see that he's trying to figure it out too, but before he can answer me, we both see a skinny little man in dirty black pants, a ripped white shirt, and a red cloth around his waist like a belt with the most rad curved knife sticking out of it. A black patch is covering one eye, and he's climbing up the mast toward us.

Although I've only gone sailing once, I know what a mast is. It's the pole that sticks out of the center of the boat to hold up the main sail. The boat I was on before had a mast that was shiny and thin, and made out of metal, but this one is wood, and huge like a tree trunk.

I can't take my eyes off of the man climbing the mast toward us, when he shouts, "There's two of 'em, Cap'n. A half-pint and a full-grown bloke."

That's when I notice his teeth. There are only four or five of them and they're almost black. I've never seen anyone as weird-looking as that man. I wish we were back at home with Scratch. I try to remember if I brushed my teeth before we left. I notice that Dad is staring at the skinny man with the black teeth, too.

"Bring the scurvy rats down, you worthless dog's breath, before I make a meal of your other eye to the sharks." That's the captain speaking. At least I think he's the captain as I take my eyes off Mister One-Eyed Shark-Bait and look at one of the biggest men I have ever seen. The captain is huge, like one of those offensive linemen that play professional football, and I don't think he's missed many meals lately. He's dressed up in the best Halloween costume I've ever seen, with a real live monkey wearing a tiny black vest sitting on his shoulder. I can't help thinking that maybe this is a dream, or that maybe we landed in a video game. We did fall off the bluff in the earthquake, didn't we? Could heaven be a big sailboat flying a black-and-white flag? Oh, Scratch, I think, (I always talk to Scratch in my mind), is that a skull and cross-bones on that black flag?

"Throw 'em down," the captain screams, and I know now that if we are in heaven, we're on a pirate ship.

"Down the ladder, rats," Mister Black Patch says, pointing the biggest pistol I've ever seen, a pirate's pistol, at us.

"I guess we'd better go down, Rafi," Dad says.

I go first, down a rope ladder that's swinging in the wind. I didn't think it would be too hard, but the pirate ship is moving and swaying back and forth so that sometimes I'm swinging over the water. I hold onto the ropes so tight my hands are red and covered with little rope splinters when I finally get close to the deck. I don't have time to think about it, though, because two pirates grab me before I jump to the deck and start to haul me up to the captain. I can walk myself, I think, and tell them, "Hey, let me down," but the pirates only laugh, which makes me mad. I might be small, but I'm tough. I know karate. I'm a green belt. No lousy pirates are going to push me and my dad around. So I give the pirate on my left a round kick to his solar plexus. That's in the upper rib cage. He grunts, actually, he curses, but I can't tell you what he says as I kick the other one in the side with my patented back kick. He curses too and lets me go. But I've gotten myself into a bigger mess now, because he pulls out a curved and shiny sword that's as big as a baseball bat, and his yellow eyes look like they're flaming. I can see his hand tighten around the grip. It's made of tightly wound black thread. The black threads end in a tassel, but they don't cover the carved black wood face of a cat with two red rubies for eyes. Oh my gosh, Scratch, I think. I'm going to be cut in half with a sword that has your face on it.

"You cut that urchin in two and I'll hang you from the yardarm, Willie Three-Fingers."

I can't believe the captain saves me as I feel the shadow of Willie's sword on my face. I notice he really does have only three fingers. I wonder if I were nice and polite to him, would he give me that sword? Won't Matt think it's cool to have a sword with Scratch's face on the handle?

I turn then because I hear a lot of noise behind me. Dad is fighting with a couple of pirates and yelling.

"All right, Dad," I shout. This is cool. I've never seen Dad fight before, but I'm a little worried because he always gets tired fast when we wrestle in the living room. Dad suddenly gets conked on the head with a wooden stick, called a pin. I'm upset. I'm really angry, and I start to run to him, but the pirate behind me lifts me off my feet and turns me toward the captain.

"You slimy Bozo ping-pong head," I yell at him, thinking I just ranked him low.

The captain leans back and laughs. He can't stop. He puts his thick hairy fingers over his huge belly and roars. I think the monkey on his shoulder eating an apple is going to fall off, he's shaking so much. And then the rest of his rotten-teeth crew starts laughing too. This is too much. At least I can see that Dad isn't hurt. He didn't get knocked out, but still, that wasn't a nice thing to do. I hope they have aspirin for the headache I know he'll have.

"Bring the squid to me," the captain yells. His belly is shaking like a tub of jello. I hope the buttons on his shiny gold shirt pop; then I'll be the one laughing. A pirate with a gross tattoo of a naked lady on his chest and a ton of tattoos covering his arms carries me up the stairs from the main deck of the ship to the afterdeck where the huge wooden steering wheel and the captain are. It's not a bad view up here. I can look over the entire ship or turn around and see nothing but ocean. Ocean? Where's Paradise Cove? Our mobile home park? Scratch?

"Where ye been hiding, squid?" the captain asks me. He and the pirates all talk funny. You'll just have to get used to it like I do.

"I haven't been hiding anywhere. Leave my dad alone or I'll kick you," I answer. He starts to laugh again, and the monkey on his shoulder has to grab his long black hair to hang on. Even the captain's beard is shaking. I look closely and see that his beard is tied into ponytails, about eight of them. Tied to the end of every ponytail is a small pink ribbon. He must have a lot of beard hair, I think. He's wearing a thick black coat with gold buttons and gold borders. There's this cloth that looks like fancy dinner napkins poking out at his wrists. It must be the shirtsleeves of his gold shirt. I figure he must like the stuff, but I can also see that the shirt is dirty and open at the top so his milk white chest is showing, and more black hair is poking out everywhere. It looks disgusting. He's got on a wide black belt with a gold belt buckle.

When he laughs, the coat spreads open and I can see two of the coolest pirate pistols sticking in his belt, and a sword with a gold handle that is so long it makes the back of his coat stick out. He's wearing red pants, the same color as mine, but they're not sweats. He's tucked the bottoms into the top of his black boots. On top of his head is the weirdest pirate hat I've ever seen. I would be embarrassed to wear it myself. First, there's a fluffy pink feather that is so long it hangs down his back, and dangling around the edges of the hat are what look like tiny golf balls, but they're really miniature skulls. I can barely see his face with all that hair, but I can't help but notice his

eyes. They're tiny and they look mean, just like the eyes of the monkey that rides on his shoulder.

Like I said before, the captain is huge, especially since I'm so close to him now, but that's not the worst thing about him. He smells bad. I'm sure it doesn't help that he's wearing a thick black coat and it's not even cold. I don't think they have showers on this ship, because the way he smells tells me he hasn't taken one in a long time. My mom would throw him into a shower fast.

"Where did ye jump ship, squid?" the captain asks me.

"I didn't jump ship," I answer back. "My dad and I were in a earthquake at Paradise Cove. You see, we were looking for Scratch. He's my black cat, but I couldn't find him in our mailbox. . . ."

"Hold on there, squid, drop yer anchors," the captain bellows.

I notice that he looks confused. He's pulling at his ponytails, and he's not grinning anymore.

He pulls real hard on two ponytails at once as he asks me, "What's this, this earthquake, ye say?"

"Yeah, it must have been a big one. Maybe seven points on the scale. Maybe bigger than the one that hit San Francisco during the World Series," I tell the captain.

"Paradise Cove, ye says?" he asks, forgetting his question about the earthquake and squinting his eyes. "A black cat?" he adds.

"Yeah, we live in the cove. You know where it is? Maybe you could drop us off there? You see, my cat, Scratch, well, I'm kind of worried about him. Remember, I told you about him? My cat? Dad says he's a lucky cat because he has an extra toe on each foot, but I really want to get home and find him. So can you help us, Captain, sir?" I ask him as nicely as I can, but I guess I'm talking too fast because the captain is squinting at me again, and all the rest of the pirates are quiet and staring at me too.

"Avast ye, squid," the captain yells. "Willie, does ye know what this half-pint be talking about? Or what language he speaks?" he yells at Mister Three-Fingers.

Willie looks confused, then turns around for help from the eye-patch pirate who scratches at his good eye but doesn't say anything. Finally, Willie answers, "No sir, Cap'n Pinky, never heard of Paradise Cove. Perhaps they're under a spell, Cap'n."

"Hmm," the captain says, speaking into his chest and pulling at his ponytail beard.

"Your name is Captain Pinky," I say, laughing.

"Rafael," I hear Dad say in a serious tone, meaning "watch what you say." Oh-oh, I think. I gulp hard and smile my best smile.

"You don't like me name?" Captain Pinky roars, reaching for both pistols.

"I love your name, Captain Pinky, sir. In fact, my favorite color is pink." It's a big lie, but I have to be nice and get us out of this mess. Besides, I don't want us to end up as shark bait.

"Hmm," Captain Pinky answers. I barely breathe until I see his hands leave the pistols. Then I act very interested when he says, "Tell me about this Paradise Cove. Be there treasure or towns to plunder, laddie?"

I have to think for a minute. I mean, there really isn't a town at the cove. There's a restaurant, but I don't think the pirates would be interested in the "catch of the day." And I know the restaurant wouldn't serve them anyway because most of the pirates aren't wearing shirts or shoes. "Well, Captain," I say finally, "there's no towns to plunder or whatever you do with them, but I think there's buried treasure. Look." I pull the gold coin I found under the pine trees out of my shoe. The whole bunch of pirates leans in, like when you're on the playground and you get hurt and everyone crowds around.

"Let's have a look at that, squid," Captain Pinky says.

I don't want to just give the coin to him, but then I think, maybe he'll help us out if I do. Maybe he'll take us back to the cove. So I tell him, "You can have this coin if you take us to the cove."

"What?" he yells.

"You heard me," I say. "I'm not giving this to you until you promise to take us to the cove." Captain Pinky is very quiet for a long moment. He pulls at several of his ponytails again. It takes him so long to answer I begin to think that we're in worse trouble than before. Finally he answers.

"Aye, aye, matey. We'll take ye home as soon as I sets me eyes on that coin of yers." Now we're getting some place, I think.

"Okay, here it is, Captain, sir," I say as I drop it into a hand that is as big around as a cereal bowl. He looks at it for a long time, and then you know what he does? He bites it! Gross. That coin has been in my shoe all day. After the captain bites my gold coin, he smiles. He has a nice smile, I think, for a pirate. He even looks friendly. Maybe Captain Pinky's not so bad after all.

"Bring the squid's father forward, Willie," the captain shouts.

"Aye, aye, Cap'n," Willie answers. Dad walks close enough to rub the top of my head and whisper, "I think we're gonna be all right. Good thing you found that coin." Then he walks up to the captain like he's not one bit afraid and puts his hands on his hips like he's waiting for something, almost like he's bored.

"And who might ye be?" Captain Pinky asks with that voice of his that would be loud enough to quiet my fifth grade class. I notice that even though Dad is a tall, big man compared to Captain Pinky he looks like a shrimp. And I always thought that Dad had real dark curly hair, but it isn't as black as the captain's. I can see he's looking the captain right in the eye as he answers, "Carlos Pérez." Oh no, I think, he didn't even say Captain or sir. I can see I'm going to have to remind him about being polite. I guess *I'll* have to lecture Dad this time.

But the captain doesn't act upset at all. In fact, he pats Dad on the arms and shouts, "Well, good day to ye, sir. Ye be wanting me to drop anchor at this Paradise Cove, eh? Yes. I think what we'll be needing is a spot o' rum and a look at the charts in me cabin, eh?"

"That sounds about right, Captain," Dad answers.

Yeah, I think, at least he said "captain."

"Cabin boy, fetch us a bottle to me quarters," the captain shouts as he leads Dad past me and down the stairs into a door under the deck I'm standing on. Dad doesn't say anything as he passes, but he winks at me before the door closes.

It's after I hear the door shut when I first see the cabin boy. He's a lot bigger than me with blond hair, a round white face, and blue eyes. He hurries by me, no, I mean runs past me, holding a little silver tray with a bottle and two glasses on it. He's sweating and he looks nervous. He almost trips over a rope on the deck. I catch his eye, but he doesn't stop, and that's when I almost stop breathing. I swear he's Matt's twin. The only thing that's different is that he's not wearing red pants. I yell out, "Matt," but he doesn't answer. He stops for a second and gives me a funny look, and then continues down the steep stairs and through the door. This is too weird, I think, but then I realize the whole day has been weird, starting with this morning when I couldn't find Scratch. I decide to see what's up.

5

THERE'S NO ONE GUARDING me now, just the helmsman, a pirate steering the boat, and he looks like he's too busy to care what I'm doing. So I walk over to the railing and look out over the ship. It's an awesome boat, but it's not very clean. There are three masts with sails everywhere. The sails near the bottom look as big as circus tents, but the ones near the top are kind of small. The wind is strong, strong enough to make the big ship lean out over the water. The pirate ship is noisy. I really didn't think it would be, but the sails flap and there's a lot of creaking and groaning, and even the water sounds loud as it slaps against the ship's sides. It's a neat sound, but I can't stand here forever.

I check to see if anyone is watching me and then hop down the stairs onto the main deck expecting to hear a pirate shout at me, but no one does. I have to walk funny because the ship is moving and tilting to one side. It's fun. I think I'll explore while I try to figure out how to get below deck. The whole ship is painted black. The wood is thick and there are ropes everywhere, ropes tied to wooden pins like the one the pirate used to hit Dad on the head. The ropes lead up to the sails or lie coiled on the deck. There are eight great-looking cannons on each side of the ship. They are tied with thick, strong-looking ropes so that they won't move. They stick out through square holes and their mouths are pointed out to sea, of course. Each cannon has two buckets of sand next to it, but I don't see any cannon balls. I thought a ship like this would need men in the sails all the time, but there isn't even one pirate up there. I pass a group of five pirates playing cards. One thing about pirates—they all have daggers in their belts or swords. It's spooky how quiet they are. The only noise comes from the ship.

I find a door near the front of the ship, check to see if I'm being watched, and go in. It opens into a narrow passage with stairs going down. The only light comes from a skylight, but it's not much. I go down the stairs and turn a sharp corner into a large room with hammocks swinging from the ceiling. This must be where they sleep. I walk across the room and through another door. On the other side is another narrow dark passageway. There are rooms on each side, but the doors are locked. I hear a sound like something scratching and then—I can't believe it—a meow. There's a cat on the ship. I listen carefully and hear the meow again. I try some more of the doors thinking maybe the cat is behind one of them, but so far, they're all locked, except for the last one. It's a little room filled with muskets and pistols locked behind metal bars. I try to pull one out, but can't. Anyway, there's no cat here.

I leave the room and have to go through another door. This must be the galley—the ship's kitchen. There are onions hanging from strings, potatoes in sacks, and a lot of barrels. There's a big stove and next to it is a short funny-looking man with a fuzzy white beard, three gold rings in his left ear, and happy eyes. He's the darkest man I've ever seen. His bald head shines from the fire in the stove. He's holding a pipe with a long stem stuck into his mouth, and it looks like he's trying to build a fire.

"Hi," I say to him.

"*¿Qué va?* Lookee here," he says to me, smiling. "You the stowaway with the gold coin, eh?" he adds, still smiling.

"Well, it's kind of strange how my dad and I got here," I answer back, surprised that he said something in Spanish, "but I am the one with the gold coin."

"Hee, hee, hee." He laughs as funny as he looks. "Good thing for you. Captain Pinky don't harken to stowaways." He laughs some more and then turns back to the fire. There's a pot on top of the stove and whatever's in it smells good.

Suddenly, I'm very hungry. He must be able to read my mind, because he takes a bowl and fills it from the pot.

"Are ye hungry, laddie?" he asks as he hands me the bowl.

"Yeah, I'm starved. Thanks," I say as I take the bowl. He tears off a chunk of dark brown bread and hands it to me, then tells me to sit on a sack of potatoes. I use the bread like a spoon. I don't know what it is that I'm eating, but it tastes great. The cook fills my bowl again and tears off another chunk of bread for me.

"Nothing like the sea to make a *chamaco* hungry, eh?" he says smiling.

"It's good," I answer. He starts laughing again, and I can't take my eyes off of his bald head which gets all wrinkly when he laughs.

"Yer welcome, laddie. Me name's Oliver. You can call me Ollie fer short." He laughs and wrinkles his head again, and then asks me, "And what name does a rascal such as you go by?"

"Rafael," I say, "but you can call me Rafi for short."

"Oh, I will, I will," Ollie says, laughing some more.

"Hey, how come you can speak Spanish?" I ask.

"You never seen a man like me that speaks our language, eh?"

"No," I answer. He's smiling so big I can barely see his eyes.

"I come from the most beautiful island in the whole world. It's filled with trees and birds and animals like you've never seen."

"Yeah," I answer, because it's the only thing I can think to say.

"The birds sing in Spanish on my island."

"Oh yeah, right," I answer. Then suddenly, he stops laughing and turns to shout, "Boy, get your backside in here."

I don't hear anybody, but then I see the cabin boy come out from behind a barrel in the corner. He looks frightened. I feel sorry for him. I wave, just a little wave, but he pretends not to notice me.

"Bring me a spot o' rum, Matthew," Ollie says. The cabin boy disappears through a door and comes back in a flash with a bottle of rum. I figure they must drink a lot of rum. Pirates don't drink milk, I'm sure.

The cabin boy hands the bottle to Ollie and is about to leave when I grab his arm. "Hey, is your name Matthew?" I ask him.

"Yes," he answers.

"This is so weird. You know, I have a friend who looks just like you, and you know what his name is?" Matthew doesn't answer. He just looks at me as if I'm strange. I can feel him trying to pull away, too, but I won't let go.

"It's all right, boy. You can talk to Rafi. Go ahead," says Ollie.

"What's his name?" Matthew asks, but he won't look at me.

"Matt," I answer, "it's short for Matthew. Can you believe it? Isn't that cool?"

"Cool?" he says, looking puzzled.

"Yeah, you know, rad, cool." They both look puzzled.

"He speaks a strange language, boy," Ollie says, winking at me. "Methinks he means it's a good-un or spot on."

"Oh," Matthew says. I guess he understands now because he smiles for the first time. I'm not sure if I understand what Ollie said, but it sounds right.

"Aren't you kind of young to be working on a ship? Don't you have to go to school?" I ask.

"School?" he says.

"School! Hee, hee, hee, hee," Ollie laughs. "The sea is his school."

Wow, I think. That's neat. Living on a ship with no books or teachers or school. My thoughts are broken by a shout. I can tell that it's Captain Pinky. His voice is louder than the P.E. teacher's at my school. Then I hear more shouting and feet running on the deck over my head.

"Looks like we'll be changing our course," Ollie says. "You might want to get topside. See the action, eh?"

"Oh, yeah," I answer. I turn to look for Matthew, but he's gone. "Thanks for the stew, or whatever it is," I say over my shoulder as I run out of the galley and up some stairs to the deck above.

I can't believe my eyes. Where did all the pirates come from? There must be a dozen of them up in the sails, and more pulling on ropes. The ship is making a wide, slow turn, and there's a lot of yelling going on. I see Dad with Captain Pinky on the afterdeck. I wave when he looks my way, and he waves me toward him. I run across the deck, leaping over ropes as I go. I feel like I already have my sea-legs. The lurching of the ship doesn't even bother me. I'm almost to the stairs leading up to Dad when I hear a blast from the captain.

"Grab the squid."

I look up in time to see Captain Pinky with a pistol leveled at Dad and a big grin on his face. The rat has double-crossed us.

One pirate makes a lunge at me, but I dodge him. I run back across the deck and make two pirates run into each other. I don't know where I'm going, but I'm not going to let them get me without a fight. I run around one mast and dodge

Mister Black Patch. I see the door to the galley. If I can make it there, maybe I can hide below. I have to dodge three pirates to make it to the door. I throw it open, only to find Willie Three-Fingers with arms spread wide. He catches me as I run into him, but I'm quick. He's left himself unguarded for a kick and, unfortunately for Willie, I kick him really hard on the shin. He yells and drops me, so I can scoot around him and down the stairs into the galley. Ollie raises his hands, wrinkles his bald head, and then points to the other door. I run through that door and down the long hallway. I figure I'm caught now, because the end of the hallway is where the pirates sleep, and all the other doors are locked. But suddenly, on my left, a door opens and Matthew pulls me inside.

"Shhh," he says, putting his hand over my mouth. "In here." He shoves me into an open cupboard. I have to crawl on my hands and knees on the floor to get into it. "Keep quiet," he says, and then closes the cupboard door. I can hear him leave as he shuts the outer door, locks it, and runs down the passageway. I can also hear Captain Pinky yelling and the pirates running on the deck above, searching for me.

I can't believe it. I'm scared, but I'm also mad. Captain Pinky stole my gold coin and lied to us. I know I've got to find a way to rescue Dad and get us off of this boat, but there's nothing I can do right now except hide. The cupboard is warm, dark, and stuffy. It must be used for sails, because I'm sitting on a bunch of them. It's large enough to sit up in, but maybe it's the heat, because after about a half hour I fall asleep.

I don't know how long I slept, but I wake to something warm and furry rubbing against my face. It scares me so much that I wake up fast and sit up even faster. I try to see what it is, but there is absolutely no light. I reach out with my hand a little, slowly sweeping it back and forth. I reach out farther and touch it. It's some kind of animal. "Rats," I scream to myself, and then I hear one of the happiest sounds of my life.

"Meow, meow."

A cat. This time I reach out and let my hand run over the cat's back until I find its head. And then I rub and rub. I can hear him purring. I feel much better when the cat comes over and sits on my lap and purrs harder. It sounds like a motor boat engine in the cupboard. I rub some more. One thing I know is that cats love to be rubbed. I make sure to scratch his jaw and around his ears. I'm scared to do it, but I have to open the cupboard door to see the cat. There's just enough light to see, and oh—I can't believe it—this cat is all black just like Scratch. This is too much! I have the weirdest feeling, and without looking, I rub my hands on his paws. You guessed it! He's got extra toes. I'm so happy that I rub his face against mine, and even kiss it a couple of times. I can't help myself. I try to decide whether I should call him Scratch or Scratch II. Finally, I decide to call him Scratchy because I think it sounds better than Scratch II. He's a very sweet cat, just like my Scratch, and he's very happy to let me rub him all over.

"Meow," Scratchy says, and I'm just about to tell him something when I hear someone at the door to the cabin. I grab Scratchy and hide under one of the sails. I'm really scared when I hear the cupboard door open and feel someone grab my leg. I expect a pirate to yell out, "I found the squid," but it's only Matthew.

"Hey, you all right," he asks, just like my friend Matt would say.

"Oh, it's you. You scared me," I say, hugging Scratchy closer. "I thought you were a pirate."

"Didn't mean to scare you, and I would've come back sooner, but the captain is having a bellyache. They've searched over the whole ship looking for you. Ollie won't tell either," Matthew says, laughing. "Here, I brought you something to eat. Sorry it's not much." He hands me a piece of bread and an old apple. The apple is spotted and feels mushy, but I'm starved.

"Thanks," I say. "How about my dad?" I ask between bites of bread and apple.

Matthew looks down at the floor for a second before he answers. "Captain Pinky had him thrown into the main hold."

"The main hold? What's that?" I ask.

"It's in the center of the ship. Well, it's big. It's what holds things, you know," he answers.

"Oh," I say, but I'm still not sure.

"The only way out of the hold is by rope. I hope your father is well. It's a slimy, deep hold, and he could've broken a leg or something when they threw him down."

"Oh, no," I say, worried about Dad.

"I see you found the kitty," Matthew says. "She's supposed to be in the hold catching rats. Sorry, I didn't want to tell you about the rats in the hold." Matthew really does look sorry. He reminds me more and more of my best friend Matt. Matt can be really nice sometimes, too. I tell Matthew I'm very worried about Dad.

He shakes his head and asks me, "You got any ideas?"

I try to think my hardest, "What if we lower a rope down to him?" I ask.

"There's two guards on the deck at all times. The captain isn't taking any chances with you still loose," Matthew answers quickly.

We both look at each other waiting for a good idea when Scratchy jumps out of my arms and runs into the back of the cupboard where it's so dark I can't see him.

"Here, Scratchy," I call. "Scratchy, here boy," I call again.

"That's a quaint name you've given her," Matthew says.

"She's a he cat," I tell him, remembering how some people think I'm a girl when they first meet me because my hair is kind of long in the back. Not that it bothers me, I just have to tell them that I'm a boy.

"Oh no, she's a kitty," Matthew answers.

Oh well, I think, it's not something to argue over. What's important is where Scratchy went. "Here, boy," I call again. "Where did he go?" I ask.

"Probably in the back, eh?" Matthew responds.

Hmm, I think to myself. "You have a light?"

"No," Matthew says, "but I can go get a candle," he adds.

"Great," I say. I watch him close the cupboard door, and then listen to him leave, locking the other door behind him. Then I hear other voices out in the passageway.

"What're ye doing in that room, boy?" I hear Willie ask.

"Nothing, sir," Matthew answers. Oh no, I think. They'll be searching this room now; I'd better hide under the sails. Just as I get to the back of the cupboard and start to pull a sail over me, I hear the door open and Willie say, "I'll bet the squid's hiding in here." I can see they have a lantern, because a little bit of light comes through a crack in the cupboard door. Oh well, I tried, I say to myself as I wait for them to catch me when all of a sudden I feel the black cat.

"Meow," he says.

"Where did you come from?" I whisper, reaching over to pet him. As I reach over, I brush against the wood at the back of the cupboard, and guess what? It moves! I push harder. There's a swinging door big enough for me to squeeze through easily. Just as I get my legs in and the swinging door closes, I hear the cupboard door open and Willie rustle through the sails. I lie as quiet as a mouse. I hardly breathe.

"Not in here," Willie says as he shuts the cupboard door.

"You're a lucky one, boy," Willie says to Matthew, and then I hear a slap and Matthew cry out, "Hey."

"There'll be worse than that when I find that squid," I hear Willie say as he stomps off down the passageway. I wait for a second until his footsteps have died off, and then I back into the cup-board and wait for Matthew.

"He didn't find you," he says, his eyes round as he looks into my cupboard.

"No! Guess what? I found a secret passageway. Actually, Scratchy found it. I'll bet that's how he gets into this room from the hold. Now listen," I say, leaning close and pulling Matthew's head close to mine. "I've got a plan."

6

FIVE MINUTES LATER, Matthew is heading out the door, and I'm on my hands and knees, with Scratchy as my guide into the secret passageway. It's so dark I bump my head a couple of times, but at least it's big enough for me to crawl in. I hope Dad can squeeze through. Most of the time Scratchy leads me by letting his tail touch my face, but sometimes he gets too far ahead and then I have to call him back as quietly as I can. When he comes back I make sure to hug and pet him.

It seems like I'm crawling forever. There are two places filled with slimy water and I think I felt a dead rat in the water. After it seems like I've been crawling for about two days and a night, I feel a blast of cool air hit my face, and then I bump into Scratchy. If he hadn't stopped, I would have fallen into the hold. Then I hear their voices. The two pirates on the deck above us are arguing. I can't hear exactly what they're saying, but it doesn't sound friendly, and there's barely enough light to see.

I look up, out through the opening in the deck and see a full moon. I lean my head past Scratchy and look down. We're about eight feet above the bottom of the hold. I still can't see my dad when Scratchy jumps down and runs through the moonlight to the far end. I hear him say, "Kitty, you've come back." I'm so glad to hear Dad that I almost call out loud to him, but I stop myself just in time.

"Dad," I whisper, as loudly as I think I can without the pirates hearing me.

"That's a good kitty," I hear him say. No, Dad, I think, this is not the time to play with the cat. Listen. Dynamite your earwax!

"Dad," I whisper, louder this time. I look down at the bottom of the hold. I could lower myself down, but what if I fall too loudly? I decide to try calling him again when I see Scratchy run into the moonlight toward me and stop. I hold my breath. Then I see my dad walking after him. I'm so glad he didn't break a leg. As soon as Dad gets close enough to touch Scratchy, the cat runs a little closer to our secret passageway. And yes, Dad follows.

When they are right below me I whisper, "Dad." He almost jumps six feet high in the air.

"Rafi, is that you?" he whispers back.

"Yes, Dad," I whisper back.

"Oh, am I glad that you're okay. You don't know how worried I've been about you," he whispers.

"Right, Dad," I cut him off. "Can you get up here?" I whisper.

"I think so. Move back." I see his hands slap onto the wood before my face, and then there he is, pulling himself up and into the passageway. I didn't think he could do it. Sometimes Dad surprises me.

"It's tight, Dad," I whisper.

"I'll follow you," he whispers back.

As we're crawling back through the passageway I feel Scratchy jump past me.

"Isn't he a great cat, Dad? I call him Scratchy."

"Shhh," Dad whispers.

When we get back to the sail cupboard, Matthew is waiting for us.

"Dad, this is Matthew. He's the one who hid me. He's cool, we got a plan to get us outta here." I say. Matthew's face turns a little red in the light of the candle.

"Thank you so much, Matthew, for helping my son and me. Now, I think you'd better blow that candle out," Dad says in a serious voice.

"I think so, too," Matthew says, blowing out the candle.

"So what's this idea you guys have come up with?" Dad asks, squinting his eyes tight.

"Listen to this, Dad. Matthew says that there's only three pirates on deck, the two who are supposed to be guarding you, and the helmsman, the guy steering the boat."

"Yeah, I know what a pilot is, sport," Dad says. Sometimes he can really be sarcastic, especially after I just saved him.

"Sorry, Dad. Well, if we wait a while, the two guards'll get tired and fall asleep as soon as they drink the extra large bottle of rum that Matthew gave them."

"Good idea," he says.

"Yeah, we thought so," I say. "Ollie is making us a sack of food and jugs of water. There's a couple of rowboats, so we'll choose one, get in it, and row away."

Dad holds up both hands and says, "Wait a minute. Where do you two think we're going to row to? Gilligan's Island? There's nothing but ocean out there."

Matthew and I look at each other. I hadn't really thought of that, just getting away seemed good enough.

"I don't know, Dad, but we're in a mess here. Besides, we have a lucky cat with us, and you always say not to worry so much," I tell him.

"I don't know. It could be very dangerous to be out on the ocean in a little rowboat," he says.

Matthew pipes up, "But, sir, it will be more dangerous when Captain Pinky catches you two. He'll feed you to the sharks. He will. You don't want to walk the plank, do you, sir?" Matthew looks so serious with his eyes wide and round and his voice almost squeaking when he says, "walk the plank," that both Dad and I swallow hard.

Finally Dad says, "Okay. We don't have a choice. It's off to sea in a rowboat. But, Matthew, can you find a sail that we might use on the boat. And we'll need muskets and swords."

"Right-o, sir," Matthew replies.

"You can call me by my name, son. It's Carlos," Dad says.

"Yes sir, Mister Carlos, sir," Matthew answers, which makes me and my dad laugh, and after looking first at me, and then at Dad, Matthew starts to laugh too.

After we've had a good laugh, Matthew points out the sails to Dad so that he can decide which one to take. Then Matthew and I sneak out of the room, down the passageway, and into the room with all the guns. Matthew has a key that unlocks the metal grates over the pistols and muskets.

"Where did you get those keys?" I ask.

"Stole 'em from the captain," he answers, smiling.

We pick out six pistols, two apiece, and three muskets. The muskets are the rifles. Matthew says we need powder. He rolls out a small barrel and grabs three bags with special spouts that he calls powder horns. These are for filling pistols and muskets. Then there's the bullets; Matthew calls them shot. They're round iron balls the size of marbles. That's what comes out of the pistols and muskets, if they work right. We drag all this stuff back to the room Dad is in to show him. It's really Matthew who shows us.

What a pain these guns are. You have to shove gunpowder and a cloth called tamping down the barrel with a metal rod. Then you shove the ball down with the same metal rod. But that's not all. To shoot the things you have to pull back the hammer and put a large sprinkle of gunpowder where the hammer hits. If you've loaded it right and the hammer makes a spark, then the gun goes off. It's a lot of work. Matthew tells us to make sure to have a good shot before we shoot. I believe him.

When we're finished loading the guns, Dad wraps everything up in a sail except for one pistol each. I really feel like a pirate now, except that I don't have anywhere to put the pistol. Now I see why all the pirates wear wide cloth belts wrapped twice around their waists.

"Are we ready to go?" Dad asks us.

"Yes, except for swords. I'll go get the swords," I say.

Dad raises both eyebrows as he says, "Okay, but be careful. I'll take care of the pilot. You two will have to take care of the guards, who I hope are sleeping. Meet you at the rowboat in ten minutes. All right?"

"Right-o," Matthew and I say looking at each other.

7

WE ALL LEAVE MY HIDING room at the same time. Matthew and Dad go toward the galley. I walk toward the door into the pirate's sleeping quarters. As I open the door I'm sure they'll all wake up, because to my ears it makes the most awful screeching sound, sort of like the seagulls at Pier Beach. I wait for a moment and then poke my head around the edge of the door. All I can hear is snoring and hammocks swinging. I tiptoe as silently as I can, grateful for the moon that gives some light. Maybe I am a little clumsy because I trip over a pirate's jug of rum and have to chase the rolling jug, bumping and bouncing on the wood deck, to stop it. I wait to breathe, praying that I didn't wake them. Then I almost jump out of my tennis shoes. There's a hand on the top of my head. I turn my head slowly and see three fingers. I count them twice, three. I'm dead, I think, but it's just Willie moving in his sleep.

I stand up and look over the side of his hammock. He's snoring and snuffling away and the sword with Scratch's face on the handle is right at his side. I start to pull it away slowly when he moves in his sleep and throws his three-fingered hand over the sword. I actually have to lift his hand to pull the sword away, and then put his hand back over his chest. I'm sweating so hard I think I need to change my shirt. After that, getting two more swords is a piece of cake.

On the way out, I find a long piece of red cloth. I pick it up, too. I start to run down the hallway to the galley, but have to slow to a walk when I almost drop the swords. I find Ollie in the galley smoking his long pipe. There's a huge cloud of smoke around his head, and although his face is serious, his bald head is still wrinkled.

"You take care, *mijo*," Ollie says to me.

"Thanks for everything, Ollie," I answer.

"Steer away from the moon and keep your course in that direction. It'll be harder for the Cap'n to see you. Here, take this bag of magic seeds. Don't laugh, my mama from the island of Cuba gave them to me. I've saved them up many a year. Maybe they'll be of use to you," Ollie says, handing over a small leather bag tied shut at the top.

"Thanks again, Ollie," I say, thinking "magic seeds?" to myself.

Ollie helps me make three cloth belts from the long piece of red cloth I brought. He ties my belt for me, sticking the bag of magic seeds tightly into one of the folds and Willie's sword against my left side.

"Good luck," he says, patting me on my head and waving as I leave the galley. I wave back quickly and run up the stairs.

I find Matthew up at the door to the deck. He's peeking out around the edge of the door.

"Shhh, they're asleep," he tells me.

"What about my dad?" I ask.

"There, he's just knocked the pilot silly. Hoo, hoo," Matthew laughs.

"Come on," I say, still whispering, "let's go."

We run out onto the deck waving at my dad who is moving quickly toward us. I follow Matthew to the rowboat. Matthew and I grab one rope, and Dad the other. "All together now," we whisper, then lower the rowboat into the ocean. Matthew throws over a rope ladder and climbs down. Dad and I tie everything into the sail and lower that down to him.

Dad says, "After you," and I start to climb over, when I suddenly remember Scratchy.

"Oh no," I say to Dad, "I've got to get our cat," and jump back onto the pirate ship.

"Rafael Pérez," Dad says sternly, but I'm gone. I run back to the sail room, but I don't find him there. Oh no, I think, Scratchy is in the hold. I run back up and sneak past the two sleeping pirates. I can hear Dad hissing at me to come back but I have to find our cat. "Here, Scratchy," I whisper into the hold.

"Meow, meow," he answers.

"Come on, boy," I call. He just licks his paws in the moonlight and looks up at me. Well, I think, there's only one thing to do. I throw a rope over the side into the hold, shimmy down it, grab him, put him on my shoulder and climb back out.

But as I'm coming up, Scratchy jumps off of my shoulder and hits the deck running. He runs right over to Dad, who is really upset. Believe me, I can tell. I climb out of the hold and, like a dummy, step on one of the sleeping pirates. The pirate jumps up and tries to grab me, but I'm too fast for him. Dad shouts "Look out!" and starts to run toward me. I turn and see the pirate aiming his pistol at Dad. Only one thing to do since I caused this mess. The flying side kick. It's right on target and just hard enough to make the pirate fall over backwards into the hold.

"Boom," goes the pistol when the pirate lands. I look at my dad, shrug my shoulders and give him a little smile, and then we both start running to the rope ladder.

"Hurry," he says to me, as if I need to be told. Scratchy and I climb down together. I'm holding him. Dad follows. We shove off from the side of the ship and start rowing for our lives. Thankfully, there's no wind to help the pirate ship, but then there is Captain Pinky.

ght to see the pirates bumping into one another and yelling at each other, but it isn't so funny when the first cannon goes off, and then five more.

It takes a couple of seconds before the cannon-balls hit the water, so at first I think they forgot to load 'em up, but when they hit, they make a splash larger and higher than Andrew, the biggest kid in school, could make from the top of the diving platform in the junior high pool. I feel like stopping to watch the cannons because it looks so neat when they go off.

First there's a bunch of fire that shoots straight out of the mouth of the cannon, and then there's an awesome boom that echoes off the water. Those cannons must be powerful because I swear I can see the pirate ship move when they shoot. I bend harder at the oars as I hear Captain Pinky's laugh and voice traveling over the water to us.

"A gold crown to the crew that drives 'em to Davy Jones' locker."

"Their aim isn't so good," I say.

"That volley was just to find their bearings," Dad says.

"The next one will be closer to the mark, meaning us," Matthew adds. He couldn't have been more correct. The next volley comes so close I swear I can see one of the cannonballs, as clear as if it were a basketball falling through the hoop, before it hits the water and drenches us. We can hear the pirates laughing, and Captain Pinky yelling for more, which makes me upset. I yell one of my worst insults at him, "Fish breath."

"Save your breath and row," Dad says.

"That was close," Matthew adds.

Scratchy starts meowing and jumps from my lap to the front of the boat.

"Watch out, Scratchy," I yell. I wonder what he's looking at in front of the rowboat. He's meowing like crazy.

"Get ready. Here comes another volley," Dad shouts. But just as he's saying it, and just as we see the pirates lighting the fuses, I feel our rowboat lift out of the water like it's on an elevator and take off. I mean, we are cranking.

"What gives?" I yell as four of the cannonballs hit the spot we just left.

Dad looks over the side of the rowboat and yells, "Dolphins!"

"Flipper," I yell.

"Mermaids," shouts Matthew.

"Meow, meow," cries Scratchy from his spot at the front of the boat.

I look at Scratchy, I look at the dolphins, I look at the rapidly disappearing pirate ship and can't believe what I'm thinking. "Dad, Matthew, it was Scratchy. He called the dolphins to save us," I tell them. Dad looks at me funny, then he looks at Scratchy and shrugs his shoulders.

Matthew says, "That cat is possessed by demons, but I like her." We all start to laugh and can't stop for five minutes. I go up to the bow and hug Scratchy who's meowing at his friends, the dolphins. Must be those extra toes, I think. A lucky cat.

I don't think those dolphins are ever going to get tired of carrying us on their backs. We keep going and going and do not slow down. Dad says we're probably going about twenty miles per hour, but it feels like sixty to me.

All we can do is hang on and watch them. They are the most beautiful fish, I mean mammals, I've ever seen, except for Scratch and Scratchy. Some swim around and under our boat and then jump out of the water. Lines of light flow over their backs and past their flippers. I think they are magical, even if Dad says it's only phosphorescence in the water. They look so smooth and happy in the ocean, like it's their playground. I don't think I'll ever get tired of watching them swim and jump in the water, but I lie down next to Matthew and Dad and fall asleep.

8

MATTHEW MUST HAVE woken up second because I feel him shaking my arm. The next thing I notice is that we're not moving any more, the sun is up, and Dad is gone.

"What, what," I sputter.

"Look," Matthew says. I look to where he's pointing. It's an island.

"Where's the dolphins?" I ask.

"Left us here, methinks," Matthew answers.

"Where's my dad?" I start to ask as I'm interrupted by a splash and Dad's wet head appearing over the side of the rowboat.

"Our own island, Dad," I say as he climbs, dripping, into the boat.

"Yes, but don't get too excited. I don't think there's any drinking water on it," he says without any enthusiasm in his voice.

"We'll explore," I say, but when I look closer I get nervous too. It's mostly sand and some grass with a big hill in the middle and a couple of smaller hills on either side of it. The island doesn't look very big, but then it doesn't look real tiny either. I gulp, feeling thirsty all of a sudden. It is hot and dry.

"Well, we've got a barrel of water," Matthew says.

"Yeah, come on, let's row in," I shout. We row in over the clearest, bluest water. It's a lagoon and it's filled with a ton of colored fish.

"Look, a turtle," I yell, and we stop to watch a huge turtle swim slowly past the boat. I'm sweating by the time we beach our rowboat and haul all of our supplies up to a jumble of rocks that Dad said will be a good place to camp. I have to jump in the lagoon to cool off. The water feels great. I'd never need a wetsuit here like I do at the cove.

After I run out of the water, Matthew and I help Dad build a lean-to against the rocks. We use the sail as a roof and the oars as posts. We tie the back of the sail to the rocks. It's not much, but it's our home now, and Scratchy likes it. We put our supplies in the shade and there's still room for all of us to fit under the sail.

This first day is neat. We explore the whole island but don't find even one spring or stream. Scratchy comes with us.

Dad makes us foreign legion hats that he ties around our heads on the second day. The cloth falls past our shoulders. He says it will protect us from the sun.

The third day we learn how to spear fish and find turtle eggs because Dad says we have to conserve our stores. He means the food we brought from the pirate ship. We don't have wood so we can't make a fire. Have you ever eaten raw fish or sucked out raw turtle eggs? Let me tell you, I may be hungry, but I could never be hungry enough to like it. Believe me, whatever my dad cooks for me when we get home, I'll eat it.

At the end of the first week, as we are sitting under our lean-to watching the moon rise over the ocean, I feel a little worried about our desert island.

"We're running out of water, boys. One cup in the morning and one at night," Dad says.

"What about Scratchy?" I ask.

"One for him, too," he answers.

I look at Scratchy. He's licking his paws and purring. He loves raw fish.

"How's the grub holding out?" I ask.

"Nothing that we can eat without a fire, I'm afraid. We'll have to eat raw fish, turtle eggs, clams, and oysters from here on in," he says. Matthew and I look at one another. I put my finger in my mouth and pretend that I'm throwing up. Matthew laughs.

"I don't know what to tell you guys. *Hasta mañana*," he says and lies down to sleep.

"*Buenas noches*," I tell him and lie down too.

"What's that mean?" Matthew asks.

"Good night," I answer. But I can't sleep. I'm too worried. I play with Scratchy for a while, but even that doesn't make me feel better. Finally I turn over on my stomach and close my eyes. I can't sleep on my stomach either because there's something lumpy poking me in the side. I reach into my cloth belt and pull out the sack of seeds that Ollie gave me the night we left. I think of Ollie for a second, then untie the bag and let one seed drop out. It's a strange-looking seed. It has a fuzzy red covering, but it's hard underneath. I lick it, hoping that it will be good to eat, but it tastes sour. I shake my head to clear the taste and put the seed in my palm so that Scratchy can taste it. Who knows? Maybe it's good for cats. He looks at it, smells it, smells it some more, and finally his slinky pink tongue wiggles out and touches the seed. He does the same thing I did: shakes his head.

"Dumb seeds," I whisper. "Magic, huh!" I stand up, walk out from under the lean-to, empty the seeds into my right hand and throw them as hard as I can over the rocks behind us.

"Good night," I tell Scratchy and fall asleep holding him.

9

I DON'T KNOW WHY I'm always the last to wake up. Dad says I'm a sleepyhead. That's true on school days, but I'm the last one to wake up this morning too. Dad and Matthew wake me up. They're jumping in circles laughing and holding hands. They've gone hyper! Looney, I think, rubbing my eyes. It's after I stop rubbing my eyes to look around that I think I'm crazy too. There's no more desert island. There are trees everywhere: banana, orange, lemon, mango, coconut. You name it, the place is loaded. And on top of all that I can hear a stream. I jump up and dance too.

"It's the seeds," I yell, "Ollie's magic seeds," but no one is paying any attention to me.

"Come on," Matthew yells. We run past the rocks under gigantic trees and into a clearing with a clear blue pool under a waterfall. I can't believe my eyes, but when Matthew dives in, I'm quick to follow. Matthew and I swim in the pool all day, and that night we have our first fire and cooked fish.

In the month that follows, I still have to rub my eyes in the morning when I wake up. I think I believe in magic now, magic seeds, at least.

With trees, the island is a paradise. I even begin to like fish, cooked, that is. With all the fruit and fish, we'll never starve. The water from the stream is also very sweet and refreshing. All sorts of birds have appeared, because of the trees, I think. I like hearing them when I wake up.

Every day isn't an adventure, even on a new tropical island, but most days are. Like the day when Matthew and I were swimming in the lagoon and I felt something rub against my leg underwater. The next thing I knew, one of the dolphins jumped out of the water right next to us. There were two of them and they let us ride on their backs. I even went underwater, holding on to a dorsal fin as hard as I could. The dolphins are such great friends. Whenever they come, they let us play with them, even my dad.

One day we couldn't find Scratchy until we heard him meowing on a limb high in the branches of a giant tree near the pool. Matthew and I climbed the tree easily by using the creeper vines. We found Scratchy in a crook, where the branches split, that's bigger around than my room back at home in the cove. That gave us a great idea.

We hauled bamboo up there and made the coolest tree fort. The best part about it is that no one can see us. My dad, I mean. Sometimes we hide up there and giggle when he calls us or walks right underneath the tree but never sees us.

We call the treehouse "Fort Scratchy," and soon we build other smaller platforms on higher branches. Those are our watchtowers, and the highest one is the crow's nest because Matthew says that's what they're called on ships. We never do tell Dad about the treehouse.

I guess Dad has fun fishing and building a house. Oh yeah, he started right after the trees grew. We have to work too. Matthew and I help every day, but Dad lets us go swimming whenever we get tired. We're building a house out of the rocks that are everywhere. We call it the "rock house." There are huge windows facing the sea and porches on all sides. Of course, we're building it right above the beach where we first camped, behind the jumble of rocks. We use palm leaves for the roof by laying them one on top of another over bamboo poles. Matthew and I get to do that part because we are so much lighter than Dad. The house is very cool. With its tall ceiling and big windows, breezes flow through our home all day and night.

We make hammocks to sleep in from dried coconut rope called hemp. Dad figures out a way to bring water to the house by making a pipe of stuck-together, hollowed-out bamboo. The pipe starts at a spring on one of the small hills behind the house. The water trickles through all the time and makes a neat sound, like a fountain, as it falls into a big turtle shell in front of one of the windows. There's a hole in the turtle shell so the water can wash down on the rocks under our house. We use coconut shells that we cut in half with the pirate swords for cups.

We press coconuts under a huge rock that takes the three of us to lift with a pole to make a kind of oil for our abalone shell lamps. I can really see why people who live on islands must love coconut trees. They are so useful.

At the end of our first month on our island I get homesick and almost start to cry up in the tree fort. I miss my mom and the cove and our mobile home. I miss my friends, karate class, Little League, and even school. I'm glad I'm alone so Dad and Matthew can't see me almost crying. I guess everyone has to cry sometimes, but I don't, not even a little bit.

Before I can finish feeling sad, I hear Matthew coming up the tree.

"What's the secret password?" I ask.

"Captain Pinky's a slimy sea slug," Matthew answers as he climbs into our fort.

"Hey, whatya want to do?" I ask.

"I don't know. Your father wants us to help him. He has a new project."

"Oh no," I say, looking at Matthew. I start laughing.

"What are you laughing about?" he asks. I have forgotten about feeling sad. All it takes is having my friend Matthew with me.

"You should see yourself," I say. "Your hair is getting long, and it's not even blond anymore, it's white. And you know what? You're almost as skinny as I am, and you're real brown."

"Don't fool me," Matthew says, suddenly serious.

"I'm not kidding you," I say, laughing.

"Well, you should see what you look like," Matthew says, laughing. "Your hair is as long as a pirate's, but it's really curly. You're not even brown; you're almost black, and your arms are skinnier than these bamboo poles."

We both start to laugh real hard and we can't stop for what seems like a half hour until we hear Dad calling us. He's right below our tree, walking slowly, and looking around, because although he can hear us he can't see us. That makes us hold our hands over our mouths and press tight to keep the laughter inside. I think that he's caught us because he looks up once, staring into the tree carefully, but then he walks away calling out, "Matthew, Rafi." Of course, not getting caught makes us laugh so much that I almost roll off the platform.

"We better go down," Matthew says, finally. As we start to climb down, Scratchy appears from up above us. He's in a big hurry. I call out, "Scratchy," but he doesn't stop as he hops from limb to limb, then races down the creeper vines and hits the ground running.

What's gotten into him, I wonder as I follow Matthew down our tree, stepping on his head twice because he's so cautious and slow. I think of Dad walking under the tree a moment ago. No one would recognize him back at the cove. He's real dark now. He's got a beard with some gray in it, and he's lost the extra ten pounds he used to like to pat on his stomach.

"Didya see Scratchy?" I ask Dad as soon as we find him at the rock house.

"He was here about three minutes ago. He was meowing and acting strange, and then he took off for the volcano," Dad answers.

The volcano is what we nicknamed the big hill on our island. We call it that for two reasons. The first time we climbed it Dad said he was as tired as the time we climbed Popo, a volcano near our friend's house in central Mexico. If you've ever been to a Mexican restaurant, you've probably seen a picture of Popo. Sometimes it's on a calendar behind the cash register but usually it's on one of those black velvet pictures that are painted with all the shiny colors. Don't worry. It isn't a live volcano; it even has snow on the top. Climbing Popo was much harder than climbing our hill because of the volcanic sand. It seemed like every time I climbed one step I would slip back two more. I think Dad was tired, climbing our volcano, because of all the bushes and plants we had to go through, and he was in the front. It was about three weeks ago when we first climbed our volcano.

The other reason we call it the volcano is that we didn't climb it only for the view. We climbed up there and gathered wood to put into a pile in case we ever saw a ship. Then we could run up the hill and light our bonfire so the ship would see it and come for us. That's the second reason why we called it the volcano, in case we ever lit the bonfire.

I'm wondering why Scratchy would take off for the volcano and I'm thinking about taking off to find him when Dad says, "There's a storm approaching."

Matthew and I run out on the porch and look at the thick dark clouds. They are coming our way fast. I feel cool air, wet with rain, hitting me in the face. We went through one tropical storm already. It was strong but we weren't scared in our rock house. I am worried about our cat, though.

"I think he'll be all right," Dad says when I tell him, and then the first big gust hits the house and shakes the roof. We all look at each other.

"Scratchy will be fine on the volcano. Remember, he's a lucky cat," Dad continues. But I'm worried, and before he can say another word, I'm out the door.

Later, when I'm almost to the top of the volcano I feel bad about running out like that. Dad is probably really worried. He might even yell at me, although he doesn't yell hard, just in a loud voice to remind me to think next time. I shouldn't have run off like that, and now the storm is ready to dump and I'm a little scared. This storm is definitely worse than the last one. Some of the trees are bending over backwards during the big gusts. The rain isn't just falling; it's bashing at me like a fireman's hose turned on full blast.

We made a trail up the volcano, but it's getting muddy and I'm slipping as much as the time I climbed the real Popo. That dumb cat, I think, as I turn my back during one of the real hard gusts. Maybe I should turn back, I tell myself, but then I swear I hear what sounds like Scratchy meowing. That's all I need. I can see the top of the volcano, and even though the storm is pushing me back, I practically run to the top.

When I get there I see the big pile of wood we gathered. I see lightning out on the ocean. Leaves are blowing by me, and even a seagull is looking for a place to land. But I don't see Scratchy. I'm starting to feel like the dumbest kid ever, but then I hear his meow.

"Scratchy," I yell. "Scratchy, here, kitty. Here, boy." And then I see his little saucer face. He's in the firewood pile. I run over to him and wait with my hands out so he can climb into my arms. He does, but then he jumps out, climbs to the top of the pile and looks out to sea.

"Scratchy, get down here," I yell in a voice that is both angry and scared. He comes down again, but jumps away from me before I can grab him. "What's the matter with you, boy?" I ask him. Instead of answering, he climbs to the top of the pile again. I don't know how he does it, because the wind is strong enough to carry him off like a Frisbee on the beach. I can see that he is looking out to sea, right into the storm. At first I can't see a thing because of the wind and rain. When it lets up for a second, I stare out to sea. It seems like the storm takes a breath for that second. It's not clear, but the clouds part just enough to let a ray of sun shine through. It looks beautiful, and then I see the ship.

"Oh, man," I scream. "Come on, Scratchy, we can go now," I call to him, happy and anxious to tell Matthew and Dad. But Scratchy is stubborn. I start to climb up the pile of wood to pull him down, but I slip as I'm climbing. I'm not hurt, just wet and embarrassed. Sitting on the ground, I take another look at the ship. It looks like it's in trouble. It only has one sail up. A small white sail on a black ship. A black ship, I think. Oh, no, it's Captain Pinky. "It's the pirates, isn't it, Scratchy?" I yell. I guess he figures that I understand, or maybe it's the lightning that strikes a tree close to us, because he runs down the logs and into my arms. He even lets me carry him, although I'm slipping and sliding all the way to our rock house.

10

"DAD, MATTHEW," I start yelling as soon as I'm past the pool. Of course, they can't hear me. The rain has really hit. It's beating down as hard as a big wave at Pier Beach. I can barely see. It's as dark as my room back at the cove with only one night-light on. Scratchy meows, looks over my arms, and then shakes his head to clear the water from his ears. I don't think it helps.

The path to the house is a stream now. There's so much water coming down that the rain doesn't even have a chance to make any ripples in the water. It's like passing through black curtains. There are palm branches flying everywhere. I have to duck to keep one from hitting Scratchy and me. I see more palm fronds in the air, dried palm fronds. The roof of our house, I think. Finally, I'm at the porch and running up the stairs, screaming, "Dad! Matthew!" The roof is gone, and worse: no one's there.

"Oh, no, boy," I murmur and press my face into Scratchy's wet fur. I sit against one of the walls to protect us from the rain, but we're still getting drenched. The poor rock house. It looks

sad without its roof, sad and empty. I hug Scratchy tighter. Where could they have gone? They don't know about the pirates. Oh, this is a real drag. I guess I'll have to spend the night alone in the rock house without a roof and in the middle of a tropical storm. The worst part is that I'm getting cold. Even though the rain is warm, the wind has cooled me off and I'm starting to shiver. I'll have to get up and walk around, but I can barely see and . . . Is that my dad calling me?

"Rafi, Rafi," he's shouting.

"Dad, we're in here!" I yell as loud as I can and jump up. I'm so glad to see him.

"*Mijo*, are you okay?" he asks, hugging me.

"We're fine. Look, I found Scratchy."

"Don't ever take off like that again," he says, getting stern now that he can see I'm okay.

I don't want to apologize at first, but then I do. I know I must have scared him. "I'm sorry, Papá (he loves it when I call him Papá)," I say. "I just didn't want to lose our cat. But, Dad, it was good that I went up anyway. Scratchy wanted us to follow him. The pirate ship, Dad. I saw the pirate ship. It's coming here. It's coming to our island."

"What?" he says, his mouth so open I'm afraid he's going to drown. "You saw Pinky's ship?"

"Yes. They're having trouble with the storm and they're going to land here. Scratchy knew it," I say. Dad hugs me again, longer this time.

"Come on," he says finally. "We've got to get out of here."

"Where?" I ask.

"To your tree fort. You sneaky little devils, I should paddle both of your tails," he says, laughing.

"Right," I answer as we leave the rock house as quickly as we can. We're just in time. A bolt of lightning hits one of the walls as we're running down the steps and explodes. It's like a bomb. We're almost knocked off our feet. When I turn back to look at the rock house, one whole wall and part of another are gone, just blasted away.

"Are we ever lucky, Dad."

"We have a cat with six toes," he says, and then we go up to the tree fort.

11

OUR TREE FORT IS DRY. While I was gone, Matthew and Dad dragged up ropes and the sail. They made the sail into a tent, tying it down tight so it barely flaps. It feels good to crawl inside.

"Hi, Rafi," Matthew says, greeting me and reaching for Scratchy in one motion. He's petting and rubbing Scratchy as I tell him about being up on the volcano and how I finally saw the pirate ship.

"Were you scared?" he asks.

"No way," I answer, but he gives me a look that says he doesn't quite believe me.

"Do you think Captain Pinky will find us?" Matthew asks, making his eyes go wide and round.

"I think it was lucky that the storm hit," Dad says, and then tells Matthew about the lightning bolt, and how it made the rock house look like it hadn't been lived in for a long time. "I think we'll be safe here for a while. You know, I never noticed you guys before, even when I looked up into the tree."

"Yeah," I say.

"We have water and food up here," Matthew says.

I look at the coconut canteens, the fruit, and the dried fish they hauled up.

"We can sneak down at night for more water," I add.

"We can spy on the pirates from the crow's nest," Matthew says.

"Yeah, Dad, we have another platform higher up in the tree that we call the crow's nest. You can see everything from there and still stay hidden," I say.

"We have to be very quiet if they land on our island," Dad answers.

"Right-o," Matthew says.

"Check this out, Dad. We borrowed an idea from you," I say.

Matthew and I both jump to show him. "It's bamboo locked together into one long tube. It goes all the way up to the crow's nest. It works perfect, Dad."

"Yes, it does," Matthew adds. "Rafi says it's our telephone, but I don't know what a telephone is." We all laugh.

"Well, I've had enough excitement for one day. I'm going to sleep," Dad says and lies down. He starts to snore in two minutes, which makes Matthew and me laugh.

"Shhh," I say shaking Dad's arm.

"Huh? What?" he says.

"You're snoring," we both say.

"Huh? Oh, right," he says. Then he turns on his side and goes back to sleep.

After we stop laughing, Matthew and I plan how we're going to spy on the pirates. I think we should sneak up on them, conk them on the head, and tie them up one by one in the night. Matthew thinks there are too many, about twenty, he says. That's nothing I think. I tell him about a great movie I saw once where the guy had to fight like thirty karate guys. Then again Dad always says it's just Hollywood, and Matthew doesn't know what a movie is.

"We could swim out and burn their ship," I tell him.

But he asks, "What would we do with all the pirates on the island with us?" I guess he's right.

"Let's go to sleep," Matthew says after we've stopped talking for a while.

"I'm not sleepy," I tell him. I'm not. "Hey, let's go up to the crow's nest."

"Naw. It's still raining. It would be dangerous," he answers, lying down.

"No it isn't. Listen, the rain has almost stopped," I say, but he's already lying down. I listen. The rain hasn't stopped, but it isn't coming down like before, and the wind is hardly blowing.

"Oh well," I say out loud and start to crawl out from under the sail.

"Don't go, Rafi," Matthew says.

"Listen for me on the tube," I say, as I scoot under the sail and head up the tree.

About half way up I wonder if this really was such a good idea. Even with the creepers, and I'm holding on to them like I hold on to my handlebars when I'm going over a jump, it's slippery. I'm about to turn back when I feel Scratchy brush past me. Well, I think, if he's going, so am I, and I continue up our tree. A little more than halfway up from the tree fort is a crook in the tree where I can rest. Some of the branches must have blown off in the storm, so now I can look out and see the sky. It's not black anymore. I can see a million stars and the moon rising over the ocean. It's so clear I feel like I could just reach out and touch the moon. I hold my hand out. The moonlight is bright; it feels warm and shiny on my skin. Cool, I tell myself and start climbing again.

I almost slip twice before I reach the crow's nest. Am I ever glad to climb up onto that tiny platform! I almost don't take a breath because the view is even neater from here. There's just a few skinny branches up here that, thankfully, didn't get ripped away by the wind. All I have to do is part them a little to see the lagoon, while above me it's pure sky and stars. The moon is just off the water and its reflection is golden. I think of the yellow brick road in the "Wizard of Oz." The golden reflection leads up to our lagoon. I wonder if the dolphins are having as much fun as I am in the moonlight.

In the middle of the lagoon is Captain Pinky's ship. It looks like a toy in a bathtub from up here. It really is so rad I almost forget to call Matthew on the tube. I take a pebble from the small pile we have stored up here and drop it down the tube. I put my ear to the bamboo because I like to hear it tumble.

"Rafi," I hear Matthew say, his voice small and echoing.

"You should come up here. It's awesome," I say.

"Can you see the ship?"

"Yeah. They anchored in the lagoon," I answer.

"God's breath," Matthew whispers. I laugh. I always laugh when he says that. I think he means, "Oh, no, look out."

"It's not funny," I hear him answer, in a hoarse whisper.

"Right. Are you coming up?" I ask.

"No," he says, and then the line goes dead; I mean the tube. He's gone back to sleep, I figure, but I don't leave for a long time. Scratchy and I watch the ocean and the moon until it's right over our heads before we start down. I hope to see the dolphins, but they don't come.

12

THIS MORNING I wake up last as usual. The sun's out, but it's strangely quiet. There are no birds singing.

"Shhh," Dad whispers. Both Dad and Matthew have their fingers to their lips in the quiet sign, and then they both point down. I look between the cracks of our bamboo platform. There's ol' skinny Black Patch, Three-Finger Willie, and one other pirate. They're carrying muskets and pointing at the ground. I hear Willie say, "it's just a varmint."

"I say it's a cat print, Willie," Black Patch answers.

"You're rummy," Willie says, and heads off to the pool.

We all breathe a sigh of relief as they leave.

"That was close," Dad whispers.

"A goal line stand," I whisper back.

"That Black Patch is as sharp as a needle," Matthew says.

"A tack," I whisper back.

"A tack?"

"Never mind," Dad whispers.

That is as exciting as the day gets. I mean, we are worse than bored. You know what it's like when you get grounded and have to stay in your room? At least there's things to do in your room, and you don't have to stay quiet all the time. We don't even see Captain Pinky. He must have stayed on the ship.

Matthew and I climb up to the crow's nest about a million times until it isn't even fun anymore. The pirates walk back and forth from the pool to the beach filling barrels with water for the ship. Not one of the pirates ever looks up into the tree. Even Dad stops being so careful.

But that night it gets good. Captain Pinky rows to shore right at sunset to where the pirates have built a camp. It isn't much of a camp, just a bonfire really. The pirates wait to light the bonfire until Captain Pinky is ready to step onto the sand. That's when we sneak down the tree.

"I want to hear what they're planning," Dad whispers when we're on the ground. "I don't want you two sneaking over there. Do you understand?" he says in his gruff voice, squeezing my shoulders to make double sure I understand.

"Oh, Dad," I whine.

"Yes, sir," Matthew says.

We watch Dad sneak off, and then we go to fill up our coconut canteens with fresh water and pick more fruit.

"This is a drag," I tell Matthew.

"You heard what your father said," Matthew answers as I lean over into the pool to fill a coconut.

"Hand me another one," I say, as I lean on one hand.

"Here," Matthew says, but I can't find his hand or the coconut in the dark.

"Matthew," I hiss, and then I feel a push from behind and hear Matthew laughing as I fall head-first into the water.

"You jerk," I whisper as loud as I can when I come up. He's still laughing.

"Hey, help me up," I say reaching out my hand. I pull him in. I'm sure Dad would skin our rear ends if he catches us because we swim for a long time. The pirates don't catch us, though. They're getting drunk, drinking rum around the bonfire. We can hear them. They sound as dorky as an adult New Year's Eve party. The more they drink the louder they get and the dumber they sound. We almost get caught, but not by Dad. I mean, it is that close. Just as we're starting up with our last load a bunch of the pirates and Captain Pinky come walking up the path toward the tree.

"Hurry up," I hiss at Matthew who's in front of me taking his sweet time, as usual. I barely get my arms over the platform and pull myself up as the first of the torches lights up the whole tree and all the bushes around it. It's really wild looking. The torches make a lot of light and smoke. I almost cough, twice. We can look down through the spaces between the bamboo and see the pirates so clearly I can read their tattoos. Captain Pinky makes them stop under our tree. He's shouting, as usual. I think his monkey sees us because he's looking up at our fort and jabbering like crazy. But that only makes the pirates laugh, and then Captain Pinky jerks his rope so hard I feel sorry for the monkey. I guess they really can't see us; at least, they never say anything or look up until Black Patch stumbles on one of our coconut canteens.

"Oh no," I whisper.

"We forgot one of our canteens," Matthew whispers back. We are both real quiet and we both hold on to Scratchy as if he will protect us.

"There's something that stinks under our feet, Cap'n," ol' skinny Black Patch says, holding up the coconut and looking around at the pirates.

They all start to laugh. Captain Pinky roars the loudest, and one pirate shouts out, "The only thing stinking is what's between your ears."

The pirates are laughing so hard and punching one another that we think they're going to drop the torches.

But Black Patch isn't shy. "If ye thinks this is coconut juice, then yer scurvy rats!" he says and with his teeth pulls out the little wooden plug we made to stopper up the coconut canteens, and with a big show lets the water run out on the ground under our tree.

That's it. We're as good as caught. Matthew must be thinking about the same because he's petting Scratchy real hard. I'm about ready to tell him that we better skinny up to the crow's nest when Captain Pinky shouts for all he's worth, which is quite a lot.

"Why, ye ignorant flea-bitten son of an egg-sucking baboon, I ought to have ye run up the yardarm. There been inhabitants of this here rock. If ye had two good eyes ye might have noticed, matey. Some poor, blasted, shipwrecked rat by the looks of it. Maybe it's ye that's afeerd of skin and bones, eh?" the captain shouts, and then stomps over to Black Patch, pulls out his sword, and slices the coconut Patch was holding in half with one sweep of his sword.

I gulp. I really thought he was going to slice ol' skinny Black Patch in two, and I think everyone was thinking the same because it's awfully quiet now.

"Methinks we need a search party to hunt up this shipwrecked dog—or his ghost. Eh, Patchy?

How are ye at finding ghosts?" Captain Pinky asks.

Black Patch falls to his knees—and I can't believe it—he's blubbering and practically crying about how he never meant it and would the captain forgive him, how he's got a poor old mother back home, and how he met up with a ghost once before and barely escaped with his one good eye and all. I almost start to laugh because I know there's no such thing as ghosts, but then I remember how I hate to walk on dark streets at night. There could be a boogeyman.

Captain Pinky just laughs, so I guess all is forgotten, but ol' Patchy gets the worst of it. He has to do most of the digging. Oh, yeah. They bury one of the most awesome treasure chests right under our tree. It's one of those black chests with handles on each end, two metal strips going around and over the curved top, and a big old metal clasp with a giant padlock on it. We get to see what's in it too. Before they lower it in the hole, Captain Pinky has to rub his fat hairy fingers over his treasure once more.

All the pirates are leaning in to see, and if the cracks between our bamboo platform were any bigger, Matthew and I would fall through. We're squeezing so much to get a good look. It's a real treasure. There are diamonds, rubies, bracelets, and necklaces. But what I like the most are the

neat gold coins, just like the one I found and gave to Captain Pinky, the rat-faced thief.

"One of those is mine," I whisper in Matthew's ear.

"Yeah, and look at all its sisters and brothers," he whispers back.

"Yeah," I whisper. "You know what we could do with all that loot?"

"Buy our own ship," says Matthew.

"A motorcycle, you ding," I whisper.

"A motorcycle?"

"You don't know what a motorcycle is? Forget it. I can't explain it to you now. But they're so much fun. I guess I'd have to buy my dad one or else he wouldn't let me have one. You know how dads are," I say quietly.

"I don't know. I haven't seen my father since I was a wee one. I can't even remember him," Matthew says.

Maybe I'm just too excited with all the treasure, because at first I don't even think about what Matthew said. Then I feel bad and notice that he's crying. I rub his shoulders.

"Hey," I tell him, "maybe we can find your dad. We'll have plenty of money." He's still crying. "I know. We'll buy a boat and sail around until we find your dad. Okay? Doesn't that sound good?" I think he feels better. At least he's not crying anymore. I feel real bad for him, though. No

Papá. Dads can be a pain at times, but they're kind of nice to have around.

"Look," I tell him, still rubbing his shoulders, "we'll find your dad, and all of us can go sailing to Paradise Cove and we'll buy some motorcycles and teach you how to ride them."

"Cross your heart or walk the plank?" he says.

"You bet," I answer. "And you know what? We can help out some other people, too. There's lots of homeless people in L.A., near where I live. We can give them some money so they can have something to eat."

"Homeless?" Matthew asks.

"Yeah, there's all these really poor people who have to live in cardboard boxes. They don't have anything, but once I played ping pong with a bunch of them, and they were real nice."

That starts both of us off on things we can do for people we know or want to help. We even decide to buy Ollie a restaurant. I don't know why, but it makes us both feel a lot better.

Then we stop talking and watch as Captain Pinky closes up the chest and they lower it in the hole that Patch had to dig. Black Patch has to fill in the hole too. As soon as it's all covered, they return to their fire. They must want to celebrate more.

"Come on," I say to Matthew after they've returned to the bonfire. "Let's haul up to the crow's nest."

"Aye, aye," Matthew answers, sounding like one of the pirates.

We can see the bonfire pretty good from our nest, even though it's as far away as the other end of a football field. We can see Captain Pinky standing at the fire facing us. He's wearing his usual costume, talking all the time in that voice that's more like a shout, and feeding that poor monkey cups of rum. We both feel sorry for the monkey. Poor guy. The pirates want to see him get drunk. We both pet Scratchy a lot, and I lean over and tell him, "Don't you worry, boy. We would never treat you that way." Matthew agrees and says, "A pox on them."

I have to ask what he means.

"The pox is a terrible sickness," he tells me.

"A sickness? You mean a disease?"

"No, it's a plague. Don't you know what I'm talking about, Rafi? Red sores cover yer body. People die from it," he tells me.

"You mean chicken pox? Oh, that isn't so bad. I had it already," I tell him.

Matthew moves away from me. I can see that his eyes are round and that he's covering his mouth with both hands. "You survived the pox?" he asks through his covered mouth.

"Yeah, it wasn't so bad. I got to stay home at my mom's for a whole week. A whole week out of school," I say excitedly. "I got to stay in bed and watch T.V. and play video games the whole time. Look, I only got one pockmark from it. That's because I wouldn't stop scratching it. Here, look," I say, pointing to the pockmark, which is sort of a little hole in my skin under my right ear.

"Protect me, Holy Mother," Matthew says, but finally he looks at my pockmark, and after ten minutes of explaining to him how all the kids get chicken pox, but no one ever dies, he touches it. I can tell he's confused. Of course, so am I. His world is so different from mine, but it's not boring. I mean, he gets to sail around on a pirate ship and miss school. But then, he doesn't know what bikes or boogie boards or video games are. I wish I had my boogie with me. We would have a great time on the beach if the pirates weren't here. He's still having a hard time understanding about immunizations, and I can't believe that lots of people die from chicken pox. He keeps staring at his finger, the one that touched my pockmark, and then rubbing it on his shirt as if to wipe away germs.

"Don't worry, Matthew," I say. "The chicken pox is gone. It won't ever come back." I guess he believes me, or maybe he just forgets about it because we both see something good happening at the fire. The pirates have someone tied up and are pulling him into the light of the fire.

"Hey, one of the pirates must have messed up," I say.

"Captain Pinky will have him flogged," Matthew says.

"You mean whipped?" I ask, a little bit shocked.

"Cat-o'-nine-tails."

"What's that? Nine cat tails?" I ask in my most surprised voice.

"It's a whip made out of nine long pieces of leather. But at the end of every tail is a wicked piece of sharp lead. It's terrible the way it cuts into a man's flesh," he says.

"Oh, that's rad, but terrible," I say.

"I wish your father would return," Matthew says.

"Do you think he knows about the treasure chest?" I ask, not worried yet. "He's probably having a great time sneaking around. That's why he hasn't come back yet."

"Oh, no, Rafi," Matthew says in a voice that sounds like fingernails on a blackboard.

"What?" I ask, looking at him.

"It's your father," he answers, pointing at the pirates and the bonfire.

I look at where he's pointing, expecting to see my dad sneaking back to our tree. I have to look hard because I can't see Dad, though Matthew is still pointing, and then I see him. He's the man all tied up in front of Captain Pinky. Cat-o'-nine-tails, I think. Shark bait. I grab Matthew. "Come on," I practically yell. "We've got to save him."

"Hold on, Rafi."

"Whattaya mean, hold on?" I almost shout at him.

"We need a plan. What are you going to do? March over there and tell them to give your father back?" he asks.

"We've got guns," I say in my most worried voice.

"But, there's over twenty of them. We've got to have a plan. A good-un," he says, grabbing my arm.

I touch Scratchy without thinking, and then we lean in close together and start to plan our second escape.

13

WE HAVE TO WORK FAST because we're afraid that Captain Pinky will torture Dad, or worse. We come up with a plan, and although we're both nervous neither one of us shows it. I go up to the crow's nest one more time before we leave our tree fort to see how things are going back at the campfire. It doesn't look good. The pirates have laid a big barrel over on its side and have Dad stretched over it. One of the pirates has ripped Dad's shirt off.

"Matthew," I say as I jump down onto the main platform, "they have Dad tied over a barrel. We gotta go."

"Okay. The coconut bomb is ready. Where's Scratchy? We have to hurry before they start to flog your father," Matthew says.

"Scratchy. Scratchy. Here, boy," I call.

We both look for Scratchy, but we can't find him. Where can he be, I wonder. He's important to our plan. "We'll just have to go without him," I tell Matthew.

"It's a bad sign," he answers.

"Don't say that," I snap at him. "If you start to think that way, then things could go bad. Come on, we have to believe in ourselves." I grab his arm and force him to look at me. "We made it this far. We've done good. Look at our island, this tree fort. Remember how we escaped once before? My karate teacher says, 'you have to believe in yourself first. Believing in yourself, your power, is more important than physical strength.' That's why little guys can beat bigger guys, because they believe in themselves, and they use their smarts. You know what I mean?"

"No, and we don't have the lucky cat," he answers, but then he looks at me and continues, "But we have a good plan, Rafi."

"Yeah. All right. Slap me five," I say, holding my palm up high. Matthew slaps me five (I taught him that when we first built Fort Scratchy), and we both smile.

The most difficult part of our plan is the coconut bomb. We have to be very careful with it because it's filled with gunpowder. That was Matthew's idea. We packed a coconut with gunpowder from one of the powder horns. It was hard because the hole, one of the eyes at the top of the coconut, was really small. When we had it filled, we stuck a piece of rope in for a fuse. Matthew covered the short fuse with gunpowder. He said that would make it burn faster.

We're a little worried that our coconut bomb might not go off because the inside of the coconut is wet, but Matthew says it might not matter because we put so much powder in it.

We look around for Scratchy once more and then start down the tree. I'm very careful climbing down the tree with our coconut bomb. Matthew is waiting for me at the bottom of our tree. He went down first in case I dropped the coconut.

"What about the treasure?" I ask, looking at the fresh mound of dirt.

"We'll have to leave it. There's no time," Matthew answers.

"Right. Forget it. Let's go," I say, and we take off as quietly as we can toward the bonfire. We head through the jungle on a narrow path that only Matthew and I know about. It's slow, but we know it will hide us better than the beach. We can hear the pirates the whole time. They're noisier than ever, but we can't see them for about ten minutes because the jungle is so thick. I trip over a vine and almost drop the coconut. Matthew helps me up and whispers, "Are you okay?"

"Yeah, that was close," I whisper back.

I think it takes us about fifteen minutes to get to a hiding place. At least I think it's only fifteen minutes, because I can never tell time when I'm excited or worried. We are right at the edge of the jungle, where it meets with the beach. The pirates are not more than ten feet away. Some are so close I feel like I could reach out and scratch their ears. Matthew points upward. Are we ever lucky! There is a huge tree above us, and one of its branches almost crosses over the pirates' bonfire.

We've got to hurry now. The pirates have ropes tied to Dad's arms and legs so that they can stretch him tight over the barrel, and Willie Three-Fingers is practicing with a whip, the dreaded cat-o'-nine-tails. He's swinging it against a water-soaked log on the beach, and when the tails hit, I can see pieces of wood fly off the log.

Matthew and I touch our palms and slide them together in a quiet "high-five" gesture and I start up the tree. But before I even get up to the first branch, I hear a meow that makes my heart beat happily. Then I feel Scratchy rubbing against my face.

"You little saucer face," I whisper and start back down the tree. Scratchy follows.

"What are you doing?" Matthew whispers. Then he sees Scratchy and reaches out for him. Scratchy jumps into his arms.

"Now our plan is complete," I whisper and start back up the tree. I climb fast because I can see that Willie is finished at the log on the beach and is walking over to the barrel where Dad is tied down. All the pirates kind of get quiet for a minute. I have to be careful because I don't want to make a sound, and I'm not even at the branch that goes over the bonfire yet.

Captain Pinky starts to yell. I'm able to get up to the branch except that I shouldn't have been moving so fast because I almost drop the bomb.

"Well, lads, I say we have a drink to Master Willie here before he flogs the truth out of this scurvy rat, eh?" All the pirates yell. One jumps up and brings a cup of rum to Willie, who doesn't even bother to salute Captain Pinky as he downs the whole cup in one swallow.

"Aye, aye," he shouts and tosses the cup over his shoulder.

I whisper to myself. "Now, boy," but I don't see Scratchy. It's getting hot up here from the fire and my hands are sweating. I start to feel myself slipping, even though I have my legs wrapped as tight as I can around the tree branch. "Come on, Matthew," I whisper. "It's hot up here, and I'm gonna slip and fall on one of the pirates if you don't hurry."

Willie walks over to Dad. He's swinging the cat-o'-nine-tails around his head, making them swish loudly over the fire. I can see sweat shining on Dad's back. "Hold 'im tight, mateys," Willie tells the pirates holding the ropes. He's swinging the whip real fast now, and just as he's about to bring it down on Dad's back, Scratchy leaps into the light of the fire and lands on Dad's back. I'm so happy to see that skinny, black, six-toed cat, I almost slip and fall. All the pirates make a noise that sounds like when you're in a movie theater watching a horror movie and something really scary happens, and everyone in the theater sort of jumps and makes the same sound.

"What the devil?" screams Captain Pinky. The cat-o'-nine-tails stops swishing and some of the pirates jump back. I throw the bomb into the fire and start sliding back as fast as I can off the branch.

I hear Matthew call Scratchy in his loudest voice, and then the bonfire explodes. It's a bigger explosion than the time I dropped a sparkler into a box of fireworks one Fourth of July. The bonfire's our own private volcano. Thank God I make it back to the tree trunk, because the explosion practically blows the branch I was on into outer space. It feels like a big gust of hot wind, and then there's a ton of smoke, and I can hear pirates coughing in the dark. I can't see, but I can feel my way down the tree, and then I'm off and running to the barrel. I meet Matthew there. Dad looks a little woozy and can't talk. There's pirates lying all over the place. They're all knocked out.

14

"Dad, can you walk? We gotta get out of here," I say in my most serious voice.

"Huh, what happened?" he asks.

"Come on, Dad. Here, we'll help you," I answer. Matthew and I help him to his feet. He can barely walk, but between the two of us, we half drag him down the beach and put him into one of the boats.

"Where's Scratchy?" I ask Matthew as we climb in the boat.

"I don't know. I didn't see him after the bomb went off."

"I've got to go find him," I say, and start running back to the pirates. I can hear Matthew yell something, but I don't pay any attention.

The fire is completely out, but the moon is up. There are still pirates lying everywhere, but some of them are starting to sit up and make moaning noises. As I pick my way through and over the pirates, I call out, "Scratchy, here, boy." As I'm calling, I hear a sound that gives me goose bumps on my back. It's Captain Pinky, and he's trying to yell.

"Scratchy, here, boy," I call some more, but he doesn't come, and he doesn't meow back. I find the barrel that Dad was tied to, but I don't find Scratchy. The moon is bright, which helps, but there's still a lot of smoke.

I get down on my hands and knees and feel around on the sand. I touch a pirate's face and jump back. That's when I feel Scratchy's warm, furry body. Poor boy, he's lying in the sand, but he doesn't even make a sound when I rub him and pick him up. "Oh, please, you'll be okay," I whisper, as I rub my face into Scratchy's belly. "I better get to the rowboat," I think. "I can't stand here forever."

Just as I start to run, I hear Captain Pinky grunting. I'm so angry. I want to hurt him. I run over to where he's lying in the sand, pull out Willie's sword, with the ruby-eyed cat's face on it, and start to raise it. I'm shaking so much that I almost drop Scratchy. I hold the sword up for what seems a long time, thinking of what a mean person the captain is. But I can't do it and I finally just put Willie's sword in my belt.

"You're not worth it," I tell Captain Pinky. As I start to leave, my foot hits something hard that jingles. It's a bag of gold coins.

"I think I'll take these, since you stole my lucky coin," I say. I don't think Captain Pinky can hear me, but as I start to leave, he shouts, "Grab that squid," and a hand reaches out and closes around my ankle. I try to shake my foot loose, but the pirate won't let go. I'm scared to death and am about to yell when I see a piece of wood smoking at one end. I stretch out, but the pirate is pulling me slowly back. I drop the bag of coins, fall to the ground, and with all my effort, and still holding Scratchy, stretch as hard as I can until I feel my fingertips around the piece of wood. The pirate grunts a little and stops pulling, and because of that I'm able to stretch a little farther and grab the wood. It's hot, and I'm not even touching the part that's smoking. With one last big lunge I pick it up, sit up, and throw it in the pirate's face. He screams and lets go of my foot. I grab the bag of coins and run as fast as I can.

15

THE ROWBOAT seems like it's at the end of a long tunnel. I think I'm never going to make it. I feel really tired. I stumble and fall into the water. Dad pulls me out and places Scratchy and me gently into the rowboat.

"Let's go," he shouts, as he pushes the boat into the lagoon and hops in. I can hear the rows working, the water slapping at the side of the boat, Dad and Matthew grunting, but I can't hear the only thing I want to hear right now—Scratchy's little heart beating.

I want to help, but there's only two oars, and besides, I don't want to stop holding Scratchy. I bend down closer to try to hear his heart. There's a little sound, but it doesn't sound good. "Please, boy, don't die," I whisper.

"Look out," shouts Dad, and then we hear the muskets and pistols firing. I can hear them skip over the water, and one even hits the rowboat. WING, PING, PING.

"That was close," Dad says, but he doesn't duck because he knows we have to hurry to get out of here and to the ship.

"They're coming after us," Matthew shouts. We can see them piling into the other two rowboats. Captain Pinky is standing in the front of one, screaming at his men. "Look lively, lads. Bend yer backs, ye spotted old cows."

I don't care if they catch us. All I care about is our sweet black cat. I can't hear anything when I put my ear on his little chest. I rub him and kiss his head, but he doesn't move, and his little pink tongue doesn't slide out like it usually does.

"Dad," I scream, "Scratchy's dying. Please, Dad, do something. Please." I don't want to cry, but I can't stop myself. I can't help it as my tears roll into Scratchy's black fur, and I feel sadder than I've ever felt in my whole life. I don't even care if we ever get back to the cove, and I don't want another cat again. I just know nothing will ever be good again.

16

EVEN THOUGH we have a head start on the pirates, they're gaining on us. They have four men rowing in each boat and we only have Matthew and Dad in ours.

"Hurry!" Dad shouts. "They're catching up to us."

I don't really care about anything except holding Scratchy, but I know that they need my help. Before I put him down in the bottom of the rowboat, I lean over one more time, rub his face, and tell him, "You'll be okay, boy. We'll take good care of you as soon as we get to the ship. I love you, Scratchy." Then, as I'm getting ready to put him down, and I'm rubbing his face with my face, I feel something wet and rough touch my cheek. At first I think that it's a wave that splashed over the side, but when I look at Scratchy I see his little pink tongue, and then I see his eyes open. I squeeze him so hard he has to push his little paw against my face to tell me to stop, and then I hear a tiny purr. He's going to be okay.

I want to yell out to Dad and Matthew, but first I hug Scratchy once more before making him comfortable in the bottom of the rowboat. Then I yell, "Dad, Matthew, Scratchy's alive! He's gonna be okay." They both yell back and smile even though they are rowing hard.

I look at the pirate ship. It's still at least fifty yards away. Then I look back at the pirates in the rowboats, and they're only about twenty yards behind us. They're so close that I can see the white grin of the monkey on Captain Pinky's shoulder.

"Get ready to duck," I shout, feeling much better now that Scratchy's okay. I can see Captain Pinky pulling both pistols out of his belt. I turn to look at the pirate ship again. It's only about thirty yards away now, but how will we ever climb up the sides with the pirates so close? I look back at Captain Pinky. He's starting to aim both pistols.

"Duck," I shout, but just as I yell, I see Captain Pinky's boat bump up, as if it hit a rock or something. The water around the two rowboats is wild like a whirlpool, and something is smashing into their boats. It's the dolphins.

"Yahoo, the dolphins!" I shout. We all look, just in time to see Captain Pinky fall off the front of his rowboat. We all laugh.

The dolphins give us enough time to get to the pirate ship and up the sides before the rowboats can catch us. Matthew and Dad help me get Scratchy up the rope ladder. I'm worried about who's on the ship, but I don't have to worry long. It's our friend, Ollie, the cook with the shiny head.

"Catch yer wind and jump to it, lads. the captain is hard astern," Ollie says with a big grin.

I look over the side. The rowboats have made it through the dolphins and are now only about twenty feet away.

"You, there, matey, help me raise the anchor," he says to Matthew. "And you," Ollie says, looking at me, "repel all boarders."

It takes about ten minutes to haul up the anchor, and that's only because Ollie started raising it before we got on board. Some of the pirates are climbing up ropes on the sides of the ship before the anchor is finally up, the sails dropped, and the big ship starts to move. Scratchy lies down on a coil of ropes, and I run around and try to keep the pirates off of the deck.

There are about ten of them climbing up. I get rid of six of them real easy by cutting their ropes with Willie's sword. One is almost over the rail. I grab a pulley at the end of a long thick rope and swing across the deck. I hit him in the chest with both feet, and watch him fall with a splash as I swing back over the deck.

I use my swinging technique on one other pirate, and then have to grab two of the wooden pins that were used to bonk my dad on the head to hammer at the fingers of the other two pirates until they finally let go and tumble into the water. It feels like I'm playing the drums or the *marimbas* on their fingers. I can't see the other one, but I got rid of nine, so I figure he fell off on his own. I yell to the others, but only Matthew yells back.

Dad is in the sails with Ollie and the ship is really starting to turn and move. It's a rad feeling. The sails white and filled with wind, the lagoon a light blue green, the dolphins leading us out to sea, playing in the wake of the bow, and Captain Pinky and the pirates yelling and shooting at us from the rowboats disappearing behind us.

"It's great, isn't it, Rafi?" Matthew says when I reach him at the helm.

"Great-o," I answer.

"Yeah. We're free of Captain Pinky and on our way. We have a bag full of coins. Pieces of eight, gold crowns. All we have to do is find my father, and then head back to your cove." He's quiet a moment. "You'll still help me, won't you?" he adds.

"You know it," I say, as I turn and leave to go to Scratchy. He's moved to the bag of gold coins that I took from Captain Pinky. I pet him a little, and watch as he starts to clean his paws and face. Then I wave at Ollie and my dad in the sails. Matthew and I both start laughing. Dad's gonna fall off if he doesn't stop waving so hard, I think, and then I hear Matthew scream.

It's Willie Three-Fingers. He's smiling, walking calmly toward Matthew and me, and he's got two pistols in his hands. I gulp and reach slowly for my, I mean his, sword, with my right hand.

"I wouldn't do that, laddie, if I were you," Willie says, sneering and pointing a pistol at my chest. I stop.

Willie steps back and yells up into the sails, "Keep yerselves up in them sheets if'n you want to see the squids alive."

I see Ollie and Dad stop. They both look angry, but they can't do anything. I start to rub my hands together like I always do when I'm worried, but then I stop. I remember Dad said that our six-toed black cat would always be there for me, looking out for me and all of us, and I know then that I'll never give up, that Willie had better look out.

"Hard about, cabin slop," Willie yells at Matthew.

That really makes me mad. I don't like anyone calling my friend names, but Matthew has to do what Willie says, and starts to turn the wheel hard around. All of a sudden I can see the island again, and even though it's a nice island, I really don't think the pirates are going to welcome us.

Willie starts to laugh, "Har, har, har."'

It's not a sweet laugh. It's evil. I've got to think of something. Ollie tells Willie that if he'll just let us turn the boat back to sea, he can have the pirate ship as soon as he drops us off at the cove.

"Har, har, har," goes Willie. "You rats really thought you could get away, didn't you? Har, har har."

I move a foot to my left and brush against Scratchy and the sack of gold coins. "Hey, Willie," I shout, and reach down to the heavy bag. "You want this gold?" He's pointing the pistol right at me, but I decide that it's now or never.

"Look, it's filled with pieces of eight and gold crowns. You could be a very rich man," I say, as I move Scratchy out of the way and pull out a fist of coins. "Sorry, boy," I whisper to Scratchy.

Willie's eyes shine at the sight of gold. He can't take his eyes off my fist. Out of the corner of one eye I can see Dad untie a rope.

"Let's have a look at that booty," Willie says in a hoarse voice, as if he hasn't had a drink of water in a week. He gestures me over with a wave of his pistols.

"Sure thing, Willie," I say. "How about these?" I throw the gold coins in my hand high up in the air and over toward the railing. They look like hummingbirds for a long second, flicking their wings in the sun, darting back and forth. Willie watches them fly. He watches some hit the railing and the others float off into the deep blue over the side of the ship.

"Why, you," he starts to shout, but he's stopped short as Dad swings down and whacks into him. Unfortunately, Dad's aim is a little off, and he's only able to hit Willie's right shoulder, but it's enough to knock the pistols out of his hands. Dad jumps on Willie, but Willie rolls him off. We're all yelling at Dad to watch out when Willie jumps at him with his knife. But Matthew turns the wheel real hard, so that the ship lurches and Willie misses Dad, who's able to roll over and get up. But the fight isn't over. Willie has found one pistol, and it's leveled right at Dad.

"Bring me that bag of gold, squid," Willie yells.

"I can't lift it, Willie," I say, pretending that it's too heavy. I grunt a few times just to fool him.

Willie keeps his pistol aimed at Dad's chest, wipes his mouth, and starts to walk over to the stairs that lead up to the helm. When he's two steps up, he reaches out to the bag. His face is level with my knees.

"Here, let me help you, Willie," I say. Then I reach down, grab the bag, and swing it into his face. The other pistol clatters off onto the deck, but Willie's quick. He grabs the bag as it hits him and sends me looping over his head to the deck where I land with a not-so-perfect landing. In other words, I think my rear-end will be sore tomorrow.

Dad's got the pistol now, and says, "Give it up, Willie. Turn the ship back out to sea, Matthew."

The ship makes another hard turn. We hear the pirates yelling and cussing at us. Willie turns, takes three steps, and dives over the railing and into the sea.

Dad and I run over to see what happens. After what seems like a long time, Willie surfaces, but he doesn't have the bag of coins with him. I guess it was just too heavy, and he had to let it go. I'm sure that was the hardest thing he ever let go of in his life. The last we see of Willie is his head bobbing in the waves, his fist shaking at us, and one last yell. "I'll hunt ye down to the four corners of this very earth," he screams, and then he becomes a tiny speck in the water.

17

I'M A LITTLE SORRY to see our island disappear completely two hours later. I don't miss the bag of gold coins. I guess they aren't worth the trouble they caused. Of course, I'm mostly glad that we've escaped and that we're all right.

The next week is a lot of work, the most I've ever had to do. Since there are only the four of us to sail the ship, it means that three of us have to work the sails and steer, while one gets to sleep for three hours. We are all really tired after the second day, but no one complains because we work so well together, and because we're all happy to be on our way home.

It's a good thing that Ollie's here. Not only does he know how to cook, but he's the only one who knows anything about sailing. I'm glad of that, at least, because his cooking isn't the greatest. Ollie sets our course, which means the direction we sail in, teaches us about the sails and ropes, and how to steer. I learn a lot in that one week.

Ollie says we're sailing to the Americas, which sounds good to me. I hope he can find Paradise Cove, my home.

At the end of the first week, we're all starting to feel pretty good about sailing, even though we're all real tired. Then a terrible storm hits us. I can barely sleep for three days and nights. The only one who can sleep is Scratchy. I guess nothing bothers him. Ollie makes us furl up all the sails except for one little one in the back of the ship, but even that one gets blown to smithereens.

It takes two of us at a time to hold the wheel. Whenever it's my turn, I have to put on a slicker, that's a big oily raincoat, a hat, and boots. Even with all that gear on, I still get soaking wet from the waves that crash over the ship. We have to hold on to the wheel so that we won't get washed overboard.

It's on the third day of the storm that the weirdest thing happens. I'm standing watch at the wheel, holding on with all my strength while a wave washes over the ship, when I see a glint of gold roll over the deck. It's one of the gold coins! It must be one of the ones that I threw at Willie, but it didn't fall overboard. I know I shouldn't, but I have to. I run down the stairs and grab it just as another wave hits us. The wave tumbles me across the deck, and if it hadn't been for Ollie and the railing, I might have been swept overboard. All for a stupid coin! Boy, is Ollie mad, but he swears not to tell Dad.

The third night of the storm is the worst.

"If we can ride it out tonight, we'll be sailing sweet," Ollie says. He and Dad go up and tie the wheel down so that it can't turn every which way, and then they come below deck, and we tighten down all the hatches so that the ship won't leak. Ollie tells Matthew and me to try to get some sleep. I don't have to be told more than once, since I'm exhausted. I find a hammock and lie down with Scratchy on my chest. Before I fall asleep, I touch the pirate's coin in my sock.

I guess I don't know what really happened next because I sleep so soundly. I sort of remember a loud crash. The ship seems to stop and tear at something along the bottom, and then I wake up. Things are flying around. There's a lot of noise. I hear the main mast break and tumble down on the deck over my head.

"We've run aground," Ollie yells, and then something falls on me and it becomes dark and quiet.

18

"YOU'RE ALL RIGHT. It's just a bad dream, honey," I hear. The voice sounds so soothing, so familiar, so sweet. It's my Mom.

"Mom," I yell, and sit up.

"Whoa. Lie back down, sweetheart. There you go," she says, as she rubs my head.

I look around me. I'm home. I'm in my room at Paradise Cove. There's the picture, at the foot of my bed, of a guy getting tubed in a wave at Pipeline. There's my lucky horseshoe and my collection of race cars. The sun is shining, and I can hear Dad in the living room. I rub my eyes. I'm home.

"Mom, I'm home," I say, in my most surprised voice.

"Of course you are. You were very lucky, little one," Mom says. "The earthquake knocked you and Daddy down onto a little ledge. You could have fallen all the way down to the beach, but you're both safe and unhurt. Oh, I love you so much," she says, hugging me.

"Mom, that isn't what happened. We fell into a pirate ship. There was this terrible pirate called Captain Pinky, who was mean and had this big

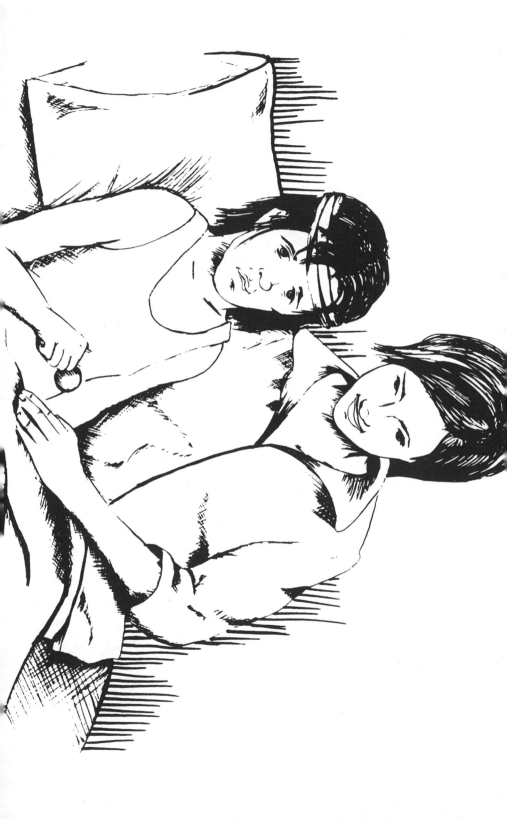

voice and a monkey on his shoulder, and this other pirate called Willie Three-Fingers 'cause he only had three fingers on his right hand, and you see, we escaped the pirate ship with a black cat like Scratch, and we found this island because of the dolphins, and there were these seeds that Ollie, the nicest man in the whole world , and . . ."

"There, there. Take a drink of water. I'd better call the doctor in and let him know that you're awake now. You were knocked unconscious for a few hours."

"But, Mom," I say, but she's not listening. She's already left the room, and I can hear her telling Dad and the doctor that I'm fine now, that I've been dreaming.

Dreaming, I tell myself. No way. I hear Dad come into the room. "There's someone here who wants to see you." Dad holds up a skinny black cat. It's Scratch.

"Dad," I yell. "It's Scratchy. I mean, Scratch. Dad, don't you remember Scratchy? We saved him from the pirates," I practically yell. I hold Scratch next to me and almost rub his ears off.

"Sure," Dad answers, quietly.

"Don't you remember Captain Pinky, and the island, and the rock house, and Matthew the cabin boy, and the little black cat that saved us."

"You need to rest. You must have been dreaming," he says.

Dreaming! Doesn't anyone remember? I pet and hug Scratch some more. "You remember, don't you, boy?" I ask. Scratch purrs back.

I think of all the cool things that happened. The coconut bomb, the dolphins, Black Patch, the pool, the volcano, Ollie and Scratchy, our tree fort. I hug Scratch. There must be some way that I can prove it. Something. Oh well, maybe everyone will think I'm crazy if I tell them the story, but at least I have my lucky, black, six-toed cat back.

The door to my room opens, and I expect to see Mom again, but it isn't. It's Matt.

"Matt," I say.

"Hey, Rafi. You all right now?" he asks.

"Yeah, I'm fine, I think."

Matt comes over to the side of the bed. "Do you remember anything, Rafi? What's it like to get knocked out?" he asks.

"Do I remember anything? Wait 'til you hear this," I say. "There were these pirates."

"Pirates! Come on, get off it. What do you think I am? Dumb?"

"No, but!!!" and then I know that I can't even tell my best friend, Matt, even if he was in the story.

"Hey, Rafi. You still got that cool coin you found?" Matt asks.

"Huh?" I answer. Then I smile as I reach down into my sock and pull out Willie's lost gold coin.